The Lonely Jacobite-
The Leprechauns

The Lonely Jacobite-
The Leprechauns

Rab Bannan

To order additional copies of this book, contact:
Xlibris Corporation
0-800-644-6988
www.Xlibrispublishing.co.uk
Orders@Xlibrispublishing.co.uk
305786

THE LONELY JACOBITE

PREFACE

This book true or false, only you my dear reader may determine the truth. There are many who will disbelieve me, so I have no misgivings in laying the facts before you, For example, go to the little town of Alvie, where at the nearby little Kirk of Alvie, 150 unconfined skeletons were discovered under the floor when the building was being restored in 1880. They were reinterned in the kirkyard with the following inscription,

'were found the bodies of 150 unconfined skeletons, who they were, where they lived, how they died tradition notes not, their bones are dust, their good swords rust, their souls are with the saints we trust'.

Do you believe in the little people, in flying saucers, in the fourth dimensional world? Do you accept theory of relativity, which Einstein proved? Well then my dear reader, believe or disbelieve, I will only narrate what happened to me and my brother, for truth is stranger than fiction.

I have written here a factual account of what took place last year. I have not exploited it, as many people would have. I am merely carrying out the instructions of the former Merlin of Scotland, Thomas Ericildoune, alias Thomas the Rhymer. I will repeat his words, "Go tell the people what they did to my Scotland" After you have read this book, go check your historical facts, see if I lie to you.

The Duke of Cumberland, the German King George's son, whose father could not even speak English was from the house of Hanover His son Duke of Cumberland was christened the Butcher, not only by the Scots for the killing of prisoners who fall badly injured on the field of Culloden, but also by his own people. The awful horrors and the atrocities in the burning, shooting, bayoneting, rifle butts, will I believe keep his name, the Butcher, alive for all time.

Cumberland was walking the field at the end of the battle when he came upon a badly wounded Highlander who spat at the Duke. He ordered the officer beside him to kill him, He refused, whereupon he called on a soldier who bayoneted him to his death. The Officer who refused was later to become famous; he was none other than General Wolfe. Lt General Hendry Hawley, reputed to be the bastard son of George 1, renowned for his brutality, frequent and sudden executions of which were his rare passion. His troops dreaded his severity. He was known to have flogged two of his officers in front of his men and they held his military knowledge in contempt. Hangman Hawley, as he was called reached Edinburgh on the 6th of January. First thing he did was build two sets of gallows, one in the Grass Market and the other in Leith.

General Huske was his second in command. Captain Bligh's men after burning Anchinarry Castle marched on westward to Moudart. Here they found the McDonalds who would not surrender. Consequently there was a great amount of execution then the awful rapings and beatings and persecutions.

Lord George Sackville, he had his baggage attacked, so he allowed his men to rape the women and bayonet the men to death. At Fort William, soldier's raided Archibauld Camerons land, left his mansion stripped, rifled then burned, taking all the contents they could carry away, His wife and five young children took to the hills, where one of his children died.

Captain Fergusson whipped one of Lord Lovat's servants till he told him where he was hiding, which by the way was in a tree, Later on the English chopped off his head.

I would like to pause here and comment on a small incident that occurred as Lord Lovat was going to his death. His jail carriage was accosted by an old women who said to him,

"You'll get that nasty head chopped off, you ugly old Scotch dog", to which he replied,

"I believe I shall, you ugly old English bastard"

Lord George Sackville took 500 men from Fort Augustus to Glen Elg. These expeditions were legendary for their brutality. General Bland ordered his commander to demolish Cameron of Lochiels house, destroy as many of them as you can', since prisoners would only embarrass him, He ordered them to burn and destroy their habitations, seize all cattle and put all men to death.

Lord Louden was different. He was scrupulous in his dealings with his prisoners who had surrendered, while Hawley disdained the human touch,

The Hangman indicated his attitude to the Duke of Richmond writing from Fort Augustus, quote,

'If in June, His Majesty would leave the foot here, and Parliament give the men a guinea and a pair of shoes for every rebel's head brought in, I will undertake to clear this country, There are many more houses to burn and I hope still more to put to death. Though by computation there are about 7, 000 houses burnt already, yet all is not yet done.'

In the last week of May, the Duke moved to Fort Augustus and from here he ordered no pacification, punishment only, carry out the order before fire and sword throughout the whole Highlands. Besides Catholic Chapels, one of the main targets were the meeting houses of the Episcopalians, Nonjuror clergy and ardent supporters of the Stuarts. Lord Anchram stripped them all of their timber to provide firewood for his troops. Those found with arms were put to death, their houses plundered and then burned. This was taking full advantage of by the blood thirsty troops who beat, stole and raped with impunity, their cattle taken, their ploughs burned and all tackle destroyed. To assist them, church ministers were told to give names of all who rebelled with a guarantee of confidentiality. This procured a great deal of parochial complications, which gave the Government an index to the Rebels throughout the country.

William McKenzie vied with Anchram in wrecking destruction between Inverness and Strathbogie, boasting that he burned the popish academy at Scala, four mass houses and two priest houses. On these occasions, I always employed Sir Harry Munro, as I know he had a particular regard for the sect, for which I have christened him, Flagellum Eccelesiae Romanae. Meanwhile, the people of Glen Morriston and Glen Garry were laid to waste.

Evan McKay caught red handed carrying letters in French was given 500 lashes to tell where they were bound, he would not. The following day 500 more still he would not tell. He was then thrown into a pit and given a pound of course meal to eat, he could not. He was then taken to Inverness, put into a Tollbooth and still he would not speak. He was then beaten with musket butts, finally bayoneted to death without revealing his secret. He is my hero.

The Glen Morriston men, a curious band of outlaws, there were 8 of them, 3 Chisloms, 2 McDonalds, 1 McGregor, 1 Grant and 1 McMillan, each with a price on their head. They lived by raid and plunder, stealing arms and food, not just for themselves but for many others. Their place of hiding was on the hills, a cave in the Breas of Glen Morriston, known as Corredhugha Gollace McBane was a giant of a man, six foot six and strong as a horse. He was trapped by the Dragoons in the aftermath of the battle of Culloden and he killed 13 men before he was finally brought down.

Young Roderick McKenzie who looked and dressed like Bonnie Prince Charlie had served as a Prince life guard in the aftermath of Culloden. He was caught skulking in the hills of Glen Morrsiton by soldiers. Badly wounded he cried out

"you have killed your Prince" and with that he died

The soldiers thought it was the Prince, cut off his head and took it to Cumberland, who was at Fort Augustus at the time. The fool that he was, packed it quickly into a case and took the coach to London, where it was found to be fake and he was laughed at for his troubles

During the Rebellion, any Officer taken prisoner by the Jacobites before being released would give their word not to take up arms against them again, this they all respected, till Cumberland came along. He asked them to fight again and in doing so, they broke their work, only a few refused.

There were 5,000 Hessians under the command of the Prince of Hesse, 1,000 Argyles and also 3000 English Troops at Culloden

To sum up the Duke of Cumberland, it was sufficient to bring slaughter, slavery, or ruin upon man and his family if he bore upon or about him any mark of Highland origin, or connection if he wore a kilt or could not justify himself in English, he carried out wholesale butchery and ruin.

Many many heroes ie martyrs to the cause were being executed, when a scheme was concocted to kidnap the Duke of Cumberland for exchange. News rushed to France for the Princes approval. He refused, for Gods Sake, why, his stupidity had already cost many thousands of lives

So now my dear reader, please come with me on a journey, an adventure of a lifetime. Come let us enter the magic land of the time warp

THE CRY IN THE WILDERNESS

On a lonely Scottish hillside, stood the remnants of a home,

once a croft that held a family, now twas empty and forlorn,

as I approached I heard a sobbing, from a grave that stood just by,

there a little girl was crying, where her family they had died,

as I approached the girl vanished, instead appeared a stone,

and the story of her family, these words were carved upon,

my father was a Jacobite, for that he had to die,

they killed off all his family, and burned his house for by,

twas the butcher Cumberlands soldiers, that put us all to death,

God have mercy on his evil soul, when he draws his last breath,

they came before the dawn had broke and took him by surprise,

then hung him on his own front gate, before my very eyes,

they killed my Ma and Brother, as they raped her by the door,

then plunged a sword through her fair neck, left her body on the floor,

they killed my little brother, as he vainly tried to run,

they pillaged burned and looted, my lovely little home,

I climbed up to the rafters, there I thought I would be safe,

but they set the house afire, so now you know my fate,

as you read this weary mortal, say a prayer as you pass by,

for I have my peace in heaven, its for Scotland that I cry.

CHAPTER ONE

On the southern end of the loch lies Glen Arkaiq at the foot of which once stood a fine castle Anchinnary, seat of Lochief, Chief of the Clan Cameron. Now all was in ruins as the tall gaunt highlander paused to survey it. A bitter weariness shook his tall lean frame. Nothing but desolation lay in the path of the butcher Cumberland since the defeat at Culloden. Fear gripped his heart for his family He would have been here sooner but had been badly wounded in the battle, what with dragging his body into the mountains, he was lucky to be alive.

Rounding a bend in the valley, a scream of fear poured from him as he started to run towards a cottage set back in the hills.

"Lord no" he shouted, "no, no", the sounds of his anguish echoed across the Glen,

"Jeanie, Jeanie" He stopped short before the cottage. Neither it nor the barn had a roof to it, the thatch having been burned leaving only four stout walls. Lying across the floor was the naked body of his wife Jean, the rats, badgers and crows had been having a feast. He fell to his knees sobbing, his huge frame shook violently as he tenderly pressed his hand on her ravaged face. Her body, which had lain for some time, was badly decomposed, He lifted his head to gaze around him. His little boy barely five years old, lay in the corner of the room next to a little girl only two years old, their brains had been smashed in with rifle butts.

"Oh, Lord why? Why did you allow this to happen" he said.

It was as he picked up his wife's body, he noticed her right hand had been severed at the wrist, but the hand, it was missing. He carried their bodies outside, then finding a spade in the burned out barn, he proceeded to dig their graves. When he had dug deep enough, he paused. Why did they cut off her hand? Did she kill one of her tormentors before she died?

He walked around the house looking for a new grave He came on it about fifty yards from his home. They had tried to hide it by throwing heather cuttings over it. The grave was shallow and a foot down he found the dead soldier. On top of his body was a hand still holding the claymore she had killed him with. He dragged the body from the grave and trailed it about a mile to where a huge pile of rocks stood, here he laid the body, The hatred for these men spilled from his claymore as he cut the head from the body, sharpening two wooden staves, he stuck one into the body and using rocks to assist he plunged it into the ground with the head impaled upon it.

He cleaned the claymore before putting it back into its scabbard. Tears blinding him, he carried his wife's hand back to be reunited once more with her body. His two children he placed side by side in her arms, wrapped in his own plaid, then whispering softly to them, he laid them to rest. Silently he filled in the grave, then drawing his claymore the fearful war cry of the Camerons echoed around the lonely valley.

CHAPTER TWO

The two boys had been trudging over the hills. They had been walking from Fort Augustus, heading for Anchinnary Castle, both were in full highland dress, complete with claymores It was to be a gathering of the Clans, in remembrance of all who died at Culloden in 1746 on the 16th of April.

It was mid-August, the sun burning from a clear blue sky,

"Why now, this isn't April", said John the younger of the two boys.

He was about 6ft in height, dark curly headed and very broad shouldered. His brother James, one year older at nineteen, topped him by 2 inches. He too had black hair, although it was inclined to be wavy,

"How would I know?", commented James.

"One thing I do know, we should have driven instead of this walking", John grinned always moaning,

"You enjoy it as much as me", James said, lapsing into Scottish dialect "Ah ken laddie, but it's these dammed midges they're right up ma kilt, Good job I'm wearing mah drawers"

They both burst into spontaneous laughter.

James said, "One thing that puzzles me is why wear the claymores, we could have sent them on, a bloody nuisance keeps bumping into my leg"

Just then in the corner of the mountain the ruins of an old cottage, trees, grass and flowers grew in every crevasse of it.

"Let's have a look", John said, and with that the two boys made their way over.

"Golly", James said "looks like no one has walked in here for some time"

They drew their Claymores and started cutting a path for themselves, then rounding a little bend, John said to James,

"See to your sword, Sir", and away they went fencing one another.

Both boys excelled in swordsmanship taken as their sport at College, then University. Laughing John put up his blade saying,

"Wow, it's much too hot for that in this gear"

They made their way into the cottage, clearing nettles and weeds that grew in abundance. James was looking at the old fireplace where there appeared to be carvings of some sort.

"Hey John", he said "look at this"

There chiselled into the rock were two symbols of planet earth. A hand came from each of them and clasped together. Below were written these strange words.

> Be careful those who pass this way, don't touch these stones or you just may visit all of your all yesterdays.

Below was a name, Thomas the Rhymer, Bard and Prophet. Beneath that, a human skull with two crossed bones.

"Wonder what he meant?", said James

"Visit all your yesterdays, strange", said John.

Looking at the carved symbols, two iron balls shaped like planet earth,

"Who was Thomas the Rhymer?" James asked enquiringly

John who had made a study of Scots history replied,

"Thomas the Rhymer was a border prophet and Bard a contemporary with Wallace. Legend says true Thomas fled to fairyland and is to return to earth when Shrove Tuesday and Good Friday change places"

With that both boys laughed aloud. Just then both boys heard a distinctive noise like a dissatisfied humph,

"What was that?" John said.

"Oh the ghost of Thomas the Rhymer, who else?", grinned James.

"Tell you what you hold that stone on the left and I the other, maybe Aladdin's Jeanie wilt appear", they both grinned.

They placed their hands on the stones. John intoned,

"Jeanie, Jeanie, come to me, send me down two cups of tea"

No sooner had the words been uttered when the sky darkened, a vivid flash of lighting and then the most awful roar of thunder. In an instant there was complete darkness, and then a deep winding tunnel appeared round and round like a whirlpool pulling them, sucking them into a whirling vortex. Then suddenly it vanished. Instead the boys found themselves standing in an old cottage and seated by the fire was an old man, long white hair cascading down onto his shoulders, dressed in a long white robe, girdled by a golden sash. At his feet was the biggest wolfhound they had ever seen. To the left of him were two small men dressed in green tunics with small caps with feathers in them. Indeed they looked like leprechauns. The old man chortled,

"Aladdin indeed"

He waved his hand and two large cups of tea appeared in the boys hands.

"You would mock me, young sirs", he said, his highland Gaelic fell like music from his tongue,

"for why in this century from whence you came, no one cries for those whom slain, they died that Scotland would be free and give each man his liberty"

As he uttered this small poem, James who was the first to recover from the shock said,

"Are you real? Are you Thomas the Rhymer?"

Gracefully the old man bowed his head.

> "That I am and you my bonnie lads are going back. So you may tell the future what they did to my Scotland,"
>
> He then quoted another verse:
>
> "No knowledge from the present may go into the past, yourselves you may just think it, but words from you won't pass, you will live each awful minute and may die before your time, but you fight for Bonnie Scotland ere the bell for you will chime.
>
> When your time from past to present comes, you must find a Loch so green, a place where Fairies, Leprechauns, can turn time on a reel. "Remember these words"' said Thomas "and some day you might go home"

There was a huge flash and the cottage vanished, Instead the boys were standing on a small knoll looking down at a large red bearded giant of a man standing before a grave, with a sword lifted to the sky.

CHAPTER THREE

The boys looked around them. They were standing on a small hill, the Loch to their right, hills rising on either side. From where they stood, they could see the burnt ruin of the castle Below to their left the cottage and standing beside what looked like a grave was a giant of a man his sword lifted to the sky howling an abominable curse on Cumberland's raiders. They paused for a moment and looked at one another They were dressed in worn out Cameron tartans, a dirk on the right side, claymore on the left, both their shirts were torn and bloody. On their head a Tammy with a white cockade, their worn out plaids wrapped around them on their arms, targe shields made of leather and on their feet deerskin boots laced halfway up the ankle. They both looked like highland warriors. Slowly without a word being spoken they made their way down towards the big man, who was still kneeling. Quietly they approached. Both felt bad intruding on a man's grief. They came within 20 yards of him when in he jumped across the grave all in one motion, drawing his sword as he gained his feet.

"Hold now, sir"" said James. "We mean you no harm"

Red Donald, his bearded face still contorted by grief said,

"Name yourselves"

"James and John Cameron", replied James "and you sir?"

"Donald Cameron", he said, putting up his sword turning once more to look at the grave.

"I will be ready after making a headstone, then we can eat and talk", so saying he started to gather small pieces of wood The boys assisted him, In no time, the fire was going. He went to the barn, pulling a large board free and retrieved an iron bar which he stuck into the fire. When it was red hot he burned these names on it: Jean Cameron, 1720-1746, wife of Red Donald, Jamie, age 5 years, Megan, age 3, killed by Cumberland's butchers, May 1746.

It took some time to do this. He had also placed on the fire a large pot of water to boil, then he made tea. Opening his small bag, he brought out a flask of whisky, which he poured into the tea in large measures. Silently, he handed the cups to the boys, then raising his cup to the sky, he said

"I give you a toast, to Charlie"

They both echoed him,

"To Charlie", feeling the hot whisky warm their bodies.

"You will be the same as myself lads just back from Cultoden. Have you any news of Lochiel?"

"No, that we have not", replied John.

"Where then would you be heading lads?"

The question startled the boys, and the voice that replied was not their own.

"We are looking for Lochiel and we are wandering about like lost souls" Tis mighty dangerous too, as them English butchers are stripping the highlands"

"Aye", replied Donald, "that they are, but we will get more of us together and fight back against that Devil from Hell"

Again the voice, that voice that was not their own replied, "We are with you Red Donald"

With these words being spoken, Red knocked out the fire, hoisted his targe onto his back with his huge war axe, his face grey with his grief, he took one last look at the grave and they were off,

"There is a place in the hills where they will never find us, Twas my dog found it for me. We will use it as a base camp as we go after Cumberland's men

Hardly a word was spoken as we set off into the hills. The air was warm and heavy with the fragrance off the heather, but we paid scant attention to either the scent or the scenery as we tried to keep up with the red bearded giant. The wooded hillside gave way to loose shale rock the higher we climbed into the mountain. The heather was alive with insects but the boys paid neither scenery nor whatever much attention as they kept up with the long limbering stride of big Red. In the distance they heard the roar of a waterfall of Achahsaul. They dropped down following the path along Loch Arkaiq, for 12 weary miles. They plodded in the wake of Big Red and it was not until they reached the head of the Loch, that he decided to stop for something to eat.

Not a word had been spoken since they had left the cottage. Below us stretched a river winding its way on into the distance.

"Where are we?" whispered James to John,

"this is the head of Loch Arkaig John, below us is the River Peen, this is the other part of Glen Peen"

"It is indeed wild looking country, bog land and boulders", said James,

As Big Red busied himself, lighting the fire to which the boys now assisted him, they had no time to talk by themselves since they had come into the past, just then from the edge of the woods they heard something moving. They must have stood on a dry stick which sounded like a pistol shot. With a quick silent motion of his hand, Red pointed for us to take cover. Following the quick movements of Red, we lifted our gear and melted into cover, at the same time drawing our claymores, the fire had not yet been lit so it did not give away our position. Silence once more reigned as we waited, We were completely hidden in the tall ferns, which I might add were alive with insects. Most of all the dam midges, they were eating us alive, but like the hardy Scots we were trying to be, we did not move. The minutes ticked by, then we heard the soft movement close by, Still we did not move. We waited on the command of Big Red, having without words being spoken, taken him as our leader. To my left in a small gully lay John, to my right, big Red. Slowly he lifted his head, then let out the most awful roar, near frightened the wits out of us. Doogal in one swift movement he was on his feet. We both rose fast beside him to be confronted by two large bearded highlanders in full war apparel. Alistair again that full throated shout, the two men stopped in the act of drawing their weapons. They rushed forward throwing their arms around big Donald so delighted to see one another.

"Wow", said Donald "seeing as how we met up like this, we have much to talk about. Three miles up in the Peen, there is a wee cave we used to go to as children. It commands a view of the whole pass. We will make for there for we have much to talk about but before we go on, these lads are with me. Thats James and John Cameron'

The big Doogal fellow eyed us both with suspicion.

"Ah havnae seen either of these two before. Lochiel never mentioned them to me,"

Even big Red turned to look at us. When again that voice from James that was not his own, but sounded like him said "We were with Gollace McBane when he got trapped by the Dragoons McBane told us to go or he would cut off our heads himself. We pleaded with him, but he was a giant of a man and he said run or die, or by the Lord I will have your heads if you don't obey me. We owe him our life"

"Aye son, I believe yee", said Doogal.

"He killed 13 of them before they finally killed him. He was a fine man", the voice from James continued "I was wounded and James was helping me. Look" my hands moved like I did not own them. I undid my shirt and there before my eyes a long sabra cut from throat to stomach that was healing.

"I'm sorry lad doubting yee", said Doogal.

"Come on Donald, lets be off. I am so hungry, ah could eat a horse"

With that we set off climbing high into the mountains on a boulder strewn ridge. We came on the cave hidden by a huge overhanging rock. If you did not know it was there, you would never have known. It was large and roomy, They dropped their gear then without a word, Donald and his two friends picked up their war axes and we followed them to bring up timber for the fire. One hour later a huge pot which was in the cave was boiling on the fire as the porridge was being made. We made ourselves comfortable around the fire. Alistair and Doogal opened their packs to reveal huge lumps of venison, then a large jug of whisky appeared. When we had eaten bowls were filled with whisky and the talk started. LT Colonel Cornwallis has 300 troopers up here from Fort Augustus. Cumberland sent his butchers to burn Anchinnary Castle to the ground and then putting every man they found to the sword the women and children are being raped, their officers let them do as they please. Word is Brigadier Mordant has 900 men who have gone into Fraser country and they are leaving nothing behind them Lord Louden has marched from Skye to Fort Augustus taking and burning everything in their path. Lord Ancheram has taken his troops to Aberdeen. God help them and that bastard William McKenzie is with them. He has burned every Catholic Church and home in Inverness and Strathbogie.

"There is a special place in hell for him", said Alistair.

The talk continued. "Cumberland is with Cornwallis, now it is he who has ordered him to burn Anchinnary and destroy as many men as possible. He said we were all vermin He shook with rage as he uttered these words, then getting a hold of himself, he continued.

"Hangman Hawley is wrecking this part of the country, I've seen suffering the like we have never known"

"I know", said Donald, "we need more men, we must fight and run, it's the only way"

More whisky was passed. I got up and walked to the side of the cave to urinate. The whisky was laying a tired edge to me but still I wanted to know what we were getting into.

CHAPTER FOUR

From my history, I knew that the English with the help of the Argyles were looting and pillaging the Highlands but not a word could I speak. Old Thomas the Merlin, had seen to that. Strangely enough I felt no fear. Earlier that evening, it had been my turn to light the one and only pipe which we all had to puff on and I burned my finger at the fire. In a way it showed us that we both had no immunity. We could live or die. In our own century it was a boy I heard of people disappearing without trace. Maybe they too had went into a time warp. I returned to the comfortable warmth of the fire.

"One more bowl", said Donald lifting out his jug.

"Aye", they all echoed to Charlie,

"Where is he?", said Donald.

"Theirs word he is with Cluny McFerson", said Alistair. "Over at Ben Adler, he's in the cage aya Cluny's Cage" grinned Donald, "that auld bugger has more tricks up his sleeve than I've had hot dinners",. They all laughed.

"We will head for Loch An Uaine. Twas there I found many years ago as a boy a cave that runs into the heart of the mountain"

"I don't like going there" said Doogal. "It's owned by the fairies themselves.

That Loch is bright green, theres something strange about that place"

"Aye", said Doogal "there is that.

"Tis" said Patrick. "The Leprechaun King lives there and the fairies dance on the water on moonlit nights, but says he tis but foolish nonsense Truth is we will use the cavern and with it we will help as many people as we can"

There was a silence.

Alistair said, "I'm with you"

"And me", said Doogal, and both boys chorused their assent.

"We will start there tomorrow said Donald.

Quietly Donald told them of his tragedy. We all felt his pain as he spoke. James undid his plaid.

"I would be proud Donald if you would accept my plaid. I will share with my brothers"

Donald stretched out his hand.

"Thank you lads, tis kindness itself

John and I wrapped ourselves up by the fire and soon were sound asleep. The morning mists stretched over the mountains and valleys, promising another fine day. As the boys unravelled themselves from the woven plaid, already the fire was blazing and a huge pot of porridge was bubbling, there, with Red Donald patiently stirring it with a stick, which had been cleaned of bark. The boys had been the last ones to rise and they hurried outside to attend to their ablutions in the nearby stream.

"A fine morning to ye lads", said Donald, grinning. "By and by, you lads slept like a couple of bairns"

"Aye, they did that", said Doogal, who was sitting on a rock by the cave entrance sharpening his claymore.

"Tis the hard drink", said Alistair, rounding the corner and catching the gist of the conversation. "It's put many a good man to sleep. It reminds me of Fingal MacGregor down at Prestonpans on the night before the battle. He somehow got hold of a keg of good malt whisky. Well now the old sod drunk that much of it that he slept right through the battle. We could not waken him at all. We found him the following day crawling about the ditch like a blind man looking for his keg of whisky, Aye that whisky has its good and bad points" and they all laughed

When we had eaten, we doused the fire, gathered our gear and were off again following the couture of the mountain keeping just below the skyline. We headed into the grim and forbidding vastness of the mountains. By mid day we were bone weary, the heather pulled against you as at times we cut across heather filled bog land. The other three highlanders moved tirelessly not once complaining, so likewise we followed their example, and as the miles rolled by, we were indeed glad of the huge bowls of porridge we had for our breakfast that morning. We now saw in the distance a huge forest, lying as it were at our feet. The pace slackened a little as we dropped down into the valley. We asked few questions lest they enquire where we came from, We listened to them conversing.

"Tis here in Glengarry forest that blind McBaig the seer lives", said Alistair, and sure enough after half an hour tramping, we came upon old

McBaig's cave set deep in the hillside. It was indeed a pleasant surprise to see how tidy old McBaig kept this cave. The walls were covered in sheepskin, small shelves carved into the rock held various implements, everything of use, indeed the cave looked warm and cosy, a cot in the corner with a table and three chairs was all the furniture, but it was spotless. He moved about like a man who could see, a huge pot was bubbling on the fire. The smell of cooking porridge made the hunger pangs in my stomach sharpen. The table was pulled to the middle as the hungry men served themselves then sat down around the fire to devour the food. The seer himself was a powerful looking character, though his back was stooped. Dressed in faded highland tartan, his face contained a deal of dignity found in few men. He busied himself about the fire, handing out extra bowls of porridge.

"Theres a flask in the corner Donald", he said, "fetch it here will you lad and we will have a dram

Donald did as he was bid, then our empty bowls were given a good measure of whisky. McBaig said,

"To Charlie" and we all echoed him as we downed our drams,

I again felt the biting warmth of the whisky, all the aches and pains of the travel vanished.

"Tis a fine whisky" said Red.

"Aye twas stolen from Lord Loudens own store"

"What news?" asked Donald

McBaig lit his pipe with an ember from the fire. It amazed me how he knew where to put his hands.

"When General Bland burned and destroyed Anchinnary, he left behind 160 soldiers and tis these 160 that have burned and raped from Loch Arkaig and all the surrounding district"

A silence settled as he said these words. Red Donald rose to his feet his eyes were sunk into his head seemed a little glazed his voice shook as he snarled,

"Where are they now McBaig, tis them that killed my family"

"Oh they will not be hard to find, they are heading over the Cairngorms and leaving a trail of destruction behind them. They are in no hurry, they pick out a place, use it as a base camp then set out to loot rape and burn. God help us, no man, woman or child is safe"

McGregor is camped over in the next valley He has 40 men with him.

"Tis good", said Red, "we will go there tomorrow and join with him"

The talk then discussed the banning of the wearing of the tartan no bagpipes, no weapons. Suddenly McBaig rose from the fire, placed his hands on each mans face till he came to James. Here he paused as his hands tugged at his shirt, then they ran his hands down the sabra cut on his chest then slowly he moved back to his place by the fire All eyes were now riveted on the old seer as he said, "I had a dream last night. I saw English soldiers dying. Those who had laid this land to waste. The lad here, your name sir?"

"James Cameron", I replied.

"You have a cut from a blade on your chest?"

"Yes sir, I have"

"Then Donald you will have your revenge in full, but you have far to travel. You are heading for the Green Loch and before the sun comes back from where it rests, your revenge will have been completed" With that he got up and left the fire,

"Tis time we laid our heads down", said Big Red, "we have an early rise in the morning"

We were laying out our plaids when McBaig whispered in John's ear,

"Thomas said your heart of times rules your head, he left this plaid for you, do not give it away, always fend for yourselves" With that he gave him a worn but good plaid. John thanked him and we ail bedded down for the night. We were up before first light, made the old man breakfast and our own. He supplied us with 2 dozen eggs hard . . . boiled. His parting words were "Find Duncan, he will take you across the Lochy" We bid him goodbye and once more were off.

They knew this land well, our comrades, as silently we made our way along hidden trails, ti! the afternoon. We camped briefly above Loch Lochy. We ate the eggs with oatcakes washed down by stream water. Donald said

"You all stay here, I will go get Duncan, we will cross in the night" and with that he departed, We wrapped ourselves in our plaids and lay down to sleep midst the tall fems and heather, not an inch of skin did we expose to the winged blood sucking enemy The stars were twinkling in their millions when we were awakened by Red Donald With him was a small squat figure of a man, who appeared to be as broad as he was tall.

"Duncan McLean lads, he will take Us across but he is not coming back. He will fight with Us"

"Aye, that I will", he grunted. "Tis sad times we have, those Red Coat bastards are raping and stealing what they want Bland left 200 men to scour this part of the mountains to Braemar They went up Loch Lochy to its head spreading out in groups stealing, killing and burning"

"We will find them" said Red "but first McGregor"

Silently we followed Duncan as he made his way down towards the Loch,

We stopped about 50 yards from the shore where Duncan started pulling at the ground. The plants came away in square blocks, Below plastered in wet peat was an upturned boat.

"Aye" said Duncan, "the peat keeps the wood swollen", then back went the peat blocks supported by straps of timber. We then slid the boat down to the water. Quietly we slid gently across the calm water. Now and again the clouds passing over the moon left us in darkness, nothing but the muffled oar locks, breaking the still silence, as we made our way over the Loch. We ground onto a sandy beach, and this time Duncan insisted we lifted the boat out of the water, We carried it Up the hillside, where once more Duncan pulled up the heather to reveal the boards underneath, upturning it we soon had it out of sight.

"It's always there when you need it, Donald", he said then we were off.

It was heavy going through the deep heather and fern, our legs were plastered in wet peat and we were bone weary. When after four hours of climbing and clawing our way up this vast glen, we had paused in a small valley of loose boulders when suddenly a voice bade us, "Lay down your arms' This we did.

Then the same voice said, "Identify yourselves?"

"Red Donald Cameron, third cousin to Lochiel himself"

With that there was a sound of swords being sheathed, and a bearded grinning figure appeared exclaiming, "Red Donald, we thought you were a dead man. Follow me lads", he said.

Out of the wraith like gloom silent men appeared. Not a word was spoken till we reached their camp in the mountains. I looked at my brother John, Lord how he fitted into all this. Indeed he looked like one of the McGregor ruffians. Little did I know 1 was of similar appearance. The camp was split up into ten sections, each having its own fire dug into hollows, the glare being screened by large ferns as was usual The fires all hung with large cooking pots. McGregor led us over to his fire, where once again the whisky was brought out, then the porridge.

"What can I do for you?", Donald McGregor asked quietly, and as big Red laid out his plan, there was a silence. All the men had gathered around to hear what was being said, his plan was simple.

"Hit all their small numbers, take no prisoners, recruit as we travel, Now these soldiers are carrying a lot of plunder, from the castle I've no doubt"

He drew a map on the ground at the edge of the fire.

"We follow them right across the mountains. Now see here is Loch An Uaine, the green loch. Well there is a cavern that runs right into the hills, big enough to hide a hundred men. You can enter one at a time. We will use it as a base camp, store anything we get, and when the winter bites deep we will hit them hard, then disappear"

"What of the plunder, how do we share?" asked McGregor,

"Every man gets the same, but if we know who it belongs to, we give it back. All except food, drink and weapons" They all agreed,

"Are you with me?" asked Red.

"Aye we are", they all chorused.

"You will be my second in command McGregor"

"Aye thats fair", says he,

"Right then lads, we move at first light tomorrow, Now tell me any news?"

"Aye Charlie is with Cluny over in the cage at Ben Adler and Cumberland's stretched his troops right across the highlands"

"Aye I know that", said Red "what of Lochiel?"

"Well now", said McGregor, "he was shot through both ankles, but where he is I don't rightly know, His cook and gardener were flogged near to death to tell them where the treasure was, but they said not a word. They then sent them off in irons to Inverness. God help them. The butcher has sent out four raiding parties from Fort Augustus to Glen Elg Cornwallis along Inverlochy with 300 men. Captain Scott and Fort William around Loch Eil, General Campbell sent to sweep everything that lies, in Sunart and Morven, and they are putting all to the sword"

"Their weakness is when they split up", said Red, "we will sweep from here to Braemar"

A tall skinny Highlander spoke up. He said, "Ewan McKay was caught with some letters written in French and they gave him 300 lashes to tell them who sent them, but not a word out of him, they took him out and put him in the toll booth and beat him to death with their musket butts. So I ask for a vote here and now. No prisoners, death to them all. Both boys tried to speak but with the power over them they could not say a word, choruses of "Aye, Aye", and so it was carried. Each one of the small band had lost someone close to them, each had his own story to tell. The sadness and anger against the English invaders, the boys knew that there would be no mercy for any one of them who fell into their hands. The words of Thomas the Rhymer came flooding back.

You will live each awful moment, and may die before your time,
but you will fight for Bonnie Charlie, ere the bell for you will chime.

The words rang in my ears, as I heard Red Donald saying, "We will start at Corriegour, my own cousin and his people are there"

CHAPTER FIVE

The evening mists were clearing as General Bland reviewed the parading of his troops by his Officers from his bedroom window at Ruthven Castle. He was what they call a book soldier, everything by the book. His troops hated him as did his Officers, but he neither cared for their affection or friendship, but tried with all his might to serve King and Country, no matter the obstacle. The Duke of Cumberland had made good use of these special qualities, in asking him to help him clear the Highlands of the Jacobite Rebels. A small knock at the door and a man entered carrying hot water and towels. Jenks his batman, a small skinny rake of a man who had served his master for countless years, not only looking after his needs but as a good ear and an informer in the lower quarters.

"Lord Louden requests you have refreshments with him, and your Officers"

Does he now", Bland said, "why do I have to suffer fools Jenks"

There was no answer, but he did not expect one. Jenks knew his place,

"Tell his Lordship, I will meet him at 9.00 a.m"

"Very good, sir", his servant replied.

He finished dressing as a small troop of six men with one Officer marched past. In front were two ragged Highlanders heading for the scaffold which dominated the front square. They were both tall and very thin, having been imprisoned for 14 days prior to the execution and Blands men did not believe in wasting food, so one meal a day consisting of a piece of stale bread and porridge gruel had kept them alive for the scaffold. One of them did not move fast enough and a soldier applied the butt of his musket to his back. He stumbled and would have fallen but his companion caught hold of him and assisted him forward. Bland stopped what he was doing to watch. No matter how many hangings you see, always something captured you to watch a man die.

He remembered these two men, captured in a raid by chance on an old farm house. They had killed four of his men, injuring three more before being taken prisoner. They would not give their names though they had both been tortured. This morning the gentle breeze blew the faded tartans hanging loosely on their ravaged frames as they approached the scaffold stairs. The soldiers kicked and shoved them to the top. Here the ropes were placed around their necks and their hands tied behind them. Bland opened his window and watched as his Officer strutted in front of the condemned men, as he held onto each minute of their last agony. They both stood proudly erect as the Officer tapped his leg with his riding crop. He said, "If one of you gives their name, I will release him" He said this in front of the tallest of the two who said something to his friend in the Highland Gaelic. His friend laughed and at the same time he spat into the face of the arrogant Officer who screamed in rage, gobs of spittle falling onto his immaculate red uniform, He slashed the Scots across the face with his whip screaming, hang the dogs, whereupon the executioner quickly sprung the traps. The two kicked out their last moments then hung still as the angry Officer wiped the dead man's spittle from his face and clothing, unaware of the smirking of his soldiers. Bland closed his window, he knew only too well the trap he and his men had got into. Instead of respect for a fallen enemy, here was hatred and the lust to kill. Under the orders of his master the Duke of Cumberland who had told him the week previous at Fort Augustus Barracks, to rid me of these Highland vermin, hunt them from their holes, hang them, don't feed them use any means you have to and bring me Charlie's head' These thoughts filled his mind as he sat down at the table with Lord Louden.

"Good morning my Lord, how are you this fine morning?"

"Oh Im well, and your good self?"

"In fine fettle", replied Bland.

"Now sir, you have news for me"

"Indeed I have sir. As you are aware, I have just come down from Skye and will join you here to assist your command with my 300 troops.

"But . . .", said Bland.

Lord Louden smiled thinly, "No buts, General, Here are fresh orders from the Duke himself'

Bland was angry, Indeed it had been his desire to march on northward, more chance of filling his treasure chests, which at the moment held gold, silver and paintings from Anchinnary Castle before it was burned.

"Now General, I have with me 60 prisoners who will travel on to Fort Augustus, As I see your justice is rather swifter than my own. Bland rose to his feet, his face pale in anger.

"Are you sir suggesting 1 am a tyrant?"

Louden rose to his feet wiping his face with his napkin.

"No General but I am suggesting your justice is rather swift"

"But", Bland said, "His Royal Highness, his own direct orders?"

"Ah yes", commented Louden, "but it is the court of God, whom some day we will all have to stand, including the Duke himself and give an account of our actions"

"I rather think General', he smiled wiping his face briskly with a towel, "we will all be found wanting on that particular day. If you will excuse me I will meet you and your Officers in the conference room"

In a few moments Bland sat down, pompous fool he thought, even the Duke could not control him. He was too fair and easy going with his prisoners, treating them rather as equals than as an enemy unlike Hawley who got himself the name of Hangman Hawley out of that man's particular lust for hanging anyone, including his own troopers, Bland remembered his comments of a letter he wrote to the Duke of Richmond. He had Jenks to thank for that. The Duke's secretary was married to Jenk's sister and she was in her own way quite fond of him, keeping him up to date with the city gossip. On this occasion he had been answering the Duke's mail from Hawley, his quote was, If His Majesty would leave the foot here and Parliament give the men a guinea and a pair of shoes for every rebels head I would clear the land, we are not here to steal for plunder I have it on good account that not only your officers, but enlisted men are filling their pockets, not counting the rapes and murders that are going on. His Royal Highness may be turning a blind eye to all this, but I assure you sirs, there is another Royal personage each of us will have to account to, who is not turning a blind eye"

A heavy silence settled on the assembled officers as Lord Louden wiped his mouth with his napkin then said, "I bid you all good day sirs", as he rose and left. All eyes were fixed on Bland who was twisting his napkin, his angry frustrated glare following the back of the retreating Lord. He would do well to remember we were in a state of war, that fellow has too much sympathy for my liking, then abruptly he changed the subject. He had always to remember Louden was a powerful figure at court Bland cleared his throat.

"At noon today, General John Huske, second in command to Lord Hawley, will be here to brief us on the overall plan for the Highlands. Meanwhile keep me posted on the amount of detachments still out. If resistance is met anywhere give no quarter to man, woman or child. His Royal Highness has issued an order that no highland dress is worn. They must have no weapons of any kind. They must speak English. Any person who fought at Culloden to be imprisoned and shipped to England. There will be 30,000 for the head of Prince Charles. Any rebel brought in must be questioned as to the Princes whereabouts. Now sirs I will have no scrupulous persons working for me, these orders must be carried out to the letter. Are there any questions?"

Not a word was spoken, they only wished he would go away and let them back to their small comforts which they all indulged in when they came in off the field. They would not even look him in the eye in case he singled them out for one of his savage attacks He let the silence build up till the air seemed to be electrified.

"What is the position of our groups, Major Hume?" instantly the Major rose at the same time lifting a sharp pointed cane. He proceeded to outline the possible whereabouts of two platoons under separate command.

"Now sir, the way I see it, the danger lies in breaking the troops into small sections, but necessary to cover the ground more quickly Each of them are due here within the next two weeks Just then the news came in of the arrival at the Fort of General Huske. He had arrived early owing to the unusually good weather conditions.

"Have him shown in immediately when he has been made comfortable. Now sirs he will give us a clearer picture"

He rang a little bell and instantly a valet appeared.

"Ask Lord Louden if he would care to join us. Tell him General Huske has arrived and tell him we will convene the meeting here in one hour"

He turned to his officers "We will reconvene here in one hour gentlemen"

General Huske, crony and henchman of the infamous Hangman Hawley was indeed a fierce looking individual, small fat pig like eyes, he looked only for faults, his great personal friendship with Hawley, each leaning on the other formed power which was felt all the way to London. The attitude towards their troops, including officers was sadistic. Hawley himself had ordered the flogging of two of his officers and had men shot depending on his evil frame of mind. They both were hated and despised by their men but fear ruled them and under their command his men robbed, raped and plundered. Failure to comply to his orders in these massacres could mean death to the soldier himself, but the English soldier always on the lookout for war booty, took to these excesses like ravenous wolves. Indeed the name Hangman Hawley become a name to be dreaded throughout the Highlands and Lowlands of Scotland.

The meeting opened, Lord Louden looking a little disgruntled at General Bland and his assembled officers, when General Huske entered, his small statute seeming to try and burst out of his tight uniform. An evil looking man in every sense of the word.

"Good day gentlemen" he said. "I am very pleased we could meet so promptly. I have with me the overall plan for the subjection of the Jacobite Rebels. Ah thank you", as he was handed a glass of claret, "it has been a tiring journey" He emptied the glass in one gulp. "Now sirs, down to business"

"As you are aware, the Duke has split his troops. Lord Anchram is at this moment wrecking destruction from Fort Augustus to Aberdeen. He has burned two libraries of popish books and all Jacobite books they have laid their hands on. William McKenzie is destroying everything between Inverness to Strathbogie. He has burned a popish academy at Scala with four mass houses and two priests houses. He is assisted by Sir Harry Munro as he knows he has a particular regard for those sects for which I have christened him, Flagellum Eccelelesia Romanae. They all laughed at that quip. Brigadier Mordan has taken 900 men into Fraser country, alongside Loch Ness. Now sirs, the Duke requests that any man found with arms be put to death. The houses of those who assist should be plundered and burnt, take the cattle, burn the ploughs and destroy all tackle. All church ministers are to be approached. Ask them to give names of all men who rebelled. You may give them a guarantee of confidence. We must weed out these vermin from their holes'

General Bland smiled for he had ordered the Commander of the men sent to Lochiels house to destroy as many of them as they could since prisoners would only embarrass him, burn and destroy their habitations, seize all cattle, put all men to death. Bland smiled at Huske.

"We sir are already doing that"

"Good good", replied Huske.

He continued. Major General John Campbell has been sent to sweep everything that lies in Snare and Morven, meanwhile Captain John Fergusson is taking his ship, Furnace, through the Western Isles hunting fugitives and all those captured are to be sent to the Tower of London.

He closed his book. "That sirs is it all. Are the men aware we are going to clean out this nest of vipers so they may never rise again?"

There was a loud hear hear from the assembled officers. Even Bland murmured his approval.

"Now gentlemen", Husks said, "1 am very tired after so long a journey. If you will excuse me"

"Of course John", replied Bland They all rose as he bowed and left. Lord Louden left with him.

Bland said, "Dismissed. See to your duties gentlemen. Keep me posted as the dispatch runners come in, is that clear? I want to know where they are and what they are doing, We will go now and see if the prisoners are now willing to speak", said Bland.

Five officers accompanied Bland as they made their way to the dungeons. They walked down a long sloping gallery, dropping down into the very bowls of the Castle, the way lit by flickering torches stuck in the side of the walls, casting their many shadows in the process, the air heavy with their odour. In the half-light two men were chained, hands and legs to the wall, large bearded Highlanders, both their faces very badly marked from heavy beatings. The one on the left was cut from forehead to chin, a vicious gash losing a great deal of blood. Lying on the floor in the corner was an unconscious figure. They opened the cell door, the smell of decayed human faeces and urine was bad, the floor littered with filthy straw.

"Do you understand Engfish?" said Bland.

No reply, just a glittering evil stare from both prisoners. Bland smiled and it sent a shiver up the officers backs for they knew the evil depth of depravity that this man could sink to.

"Fetch McTavish", he said, his commands being echoed by the officers along the passageway. McTavish a little weasel of a man who cleaned out the latrines and did other lowly tasks for the English came in on the run.

"Ask them their name", Bland said.

McTavish spoke the Gaelic and did what they asked but no reply. Just a spit from one of them.

Bland said, "Bring him over", pointing to the injured man, "let's have a look at him.

The Highlander was dragged into the torch light roughly by two soldiers. He was of medium build, about 18 years old, his shirt soaked in his own blood and it was obvious he did not have long to go unless he received medical attention very quickly even now it was probably too late, his wounds having being infected lying in filth.

"Bring him round", said Bland. The soldier applied smelting salts to the man's nose.

He groaned and opened his eyes. "Your name sir?", said Bland being echoed by McTavish in Gaelic but the Highlander who was chained shouted something to him in the Gaelic, "Say nothing lad"

A soldier hit him in the stomach with his musket butte and he bent over retching but nothing came from his empty stomach. The boys eyes rolled in pain, now glazed by approaching death. He said nothing.

"Tell him I will remove the boy's fingers one at a time, if he does not talk", said Bland.

No reply from the shackled men. Bland nodded and two soldiers grabbed the boy, one held his arm steady and the other chopped off his right hand finger. The boy screamed in agony then passed out. They brought him around again as both prisoners were throwing themselves against the chains that held them cursing Bland loudly in Gaelic, the boys breath was now coming in gulps.

"Ask again", said Bland, still no answer, Again another finger and the boys body arched in agony,

Then the boy said, "1 will tell you in Gaelic" He coughed and said something in a whisper. Blands officer knelt put his ear to the boys face to hear him. Suddenly the boy let out a roar, grabbed hold of the officers ear biting hard. The officer screamed as his ear was bitten off completely, He screamed staggering to his feet holding the side of his head. A solder kicked the boy but alas he felt nothing as he lay dead. His last act of defiance was to spit out the ear onto the boot of General Bland who recoiled in horror. It was horrific, the boy's face covered in the screaming officers blood. The faces of the chained Highlanders grinning, their own faces also masked in blood. In the flickering torch fight it was like a scene from Dantes Inferno hell on earth The Scots legs kicked convulsively then he lay still, above him his hands held to the side of his head, blood pumping out from beneath his fingers. The officer was staring wildly about him. Bland stepped back lest his uniform be stained, "Get him to a doctor", he commanded.

Two officers took him by the arms and took him away, A silence reigned as Bland looked at the two men. One of them a large black bearded individual said something in Gaelic to his companion who laughed. The big one then spat at Bland, the spit landing on his boot. No one moved as Bland removed a clean kerchief from his pocket and carefully wiped his boot.

"For the last time what is your name?"

This was repeated by McTavish. No reply.

"Very well" said he and turning to one of the guards, he said "Give me your pistol" He raised the pistol and fired the shot catching the man in the face, the ball embedding in the wall behind him. His whole body fell forward being caught by the chains. To the other orderly, he said, "Give me your pistol" He again cocked,

"Your name sir?" the question being repeated in Gaelic. He must have been prepared for it, for the spit caught Bland right in the face who being surprised fired almost without aiming, the ball catching the Scot in the shoulder, but not killing him. Spittle running down his face, Bland drew his sword and ran it through the throat of the chained man. As he drew it clear, each mans' eye was on the dying man's face then his body slumped over. Bland handed his sword to a soldier.

"Clean it and return it to me", he said to one of his soldiers. With his kerchief he wiped his face and then said, "We will go now gentlemen, our business is concluded here"

CHAPTER SIX

By mid morning the following day, we were looking down on a small settlement. At least 40 horses were corralled to the side of the small village. Now and again the flash of red as troops laughing and carousing were seen going in and out of the houses

"We cannot wait for nightfall. There must be about 50 of them down there, they don't expect trouble, no guards or any lookouts. Now by all accounts there are about 5 houses. We will leave four each side of the village, the rest we move in on when you hear the war cry And so it was, we moved like wraiths down the hillside, my stomach was churning. I glanced at John, his face tense and drawn. In what seemed like no time at all, we had taken up our positions. The cry cut through the air like a knife and there was I bursting in the door of a small cottage to be confronted by an officer's pistol coming up in one hand, sword in the other. I slashed swiftly with my sword almost severing two of his figures. He snarled a vicious oath, dropping the pistol and coming at me with his sword. He must have been up dressing, but his jacket was still unbuttoned swinging wildly about as he slashed with his sword. For a few moments he was the one who had been taken by surprise, but quickly was on the defensive. It is one thing to fence as in sport and another to live or die but before he could make another thrust with his blade, there was a loud report of a pistol as a ball caught him in the chest throwing his body over the bed killing him instantly I turned big Red grinning at me,

"Sorry lad he was yours, but we have no time to wait"

With that I followed him outside on the run. An English bowman swung our way as we left the house. He was just lining up for a shot at Big Red. I dived striking Donald with my shoulder.

"Ah" he cursed as he fell, the arrow embedded itself in the doorway I was up in an instant as the English soldier was fitting another arrow to his bow, If must have been all of 20 paces, as I drew and threw my dirk, the blade catching him just below the throat

"Twas a fine thing followed you Jamie, c'mon lad", he said.

"Wait Donald", and I ran to the bowmans body.

It was a ghastly business retrieving my dirk, which was embedded firmly, but trying not to look at the same time. I pulled it clear and cleaned it on his clothing. I turned the body over removing the quiver full of arrows, then snatching up the bow, I followed Donald back into the fray, It was over as swiftly as it had started. The surprise had effected it all, Thirty five Redcoats dead, fourteen prisoners, we lost four men in the battle, one of them who was dying. Big Lachlan asked to speak to Donald. There was a great silence in this, the aftermath of victory. The fourteen prisoners lay face down in the mud The bodies of all the rest of the dead had been pulled to lie at the side of the road. It was a horrible sight, blood everywhere. Big Red knelt down by Lachlan and cradled his head in his arms.

"Donald" whispered Lachlan,

"when you see my son Jamie, tell him I died taking four of them with me"

"Aye, that I will Lachlan, now you take it easy, you will live for a long time to come" Lachlan coughed blood spilling down his bearded chin. Then he gave a wan smile said, "Give me a dram for the road" Donald tilted the bowl and as it splashed into Lachlan's mouth he died. Gently, Big Red laid him down, removed his bonnet and placed it over his face, He rose, gently turned towards the prisoners, his face set in a terrible rage. He motioned to McGregor.

"Ask them who is in command?

McGregor kicked one fat soldier motioned him to kneel, asked him in this highland Gaelic, "Who was in command?"

The soldier did not understand a word. Red Donald said is there anyone here who can speak the English

"Aye I do" a small figure approached "I'm Colin Stewart"

He once was a humble shepherd, but his father had for some time been forced to live in the lowlands. At his heels was a collie dog which could not bark, having been attacked as a pup, and from the wounds received it would never bark again, but as a guard dog, there was none like it. Of that we will speak later.

"Ask him", said McGregor.

In soft lowland tongue Colin said, "Who is your leader?"

As he asked the question, the prisoners heads all turned looking over watchfully; The kneeling soldier grinned then spat into the ground, but did not answer. Red Donald stepped forward grasped the large soldiers' head of hair and as quick as a flash, cut his throat. The body fell forward into the mud quivering, one last kick then he was still. McGregor pulled the next one to his knees. He was indeed a mean looking individual, having served with His Majesty's army for eight years home and abroad. His own record of torment and the people he had killed had hardened him into knowing that death to a soldier was part of his life, This one laughed in the face of his tormentors.

"You bunch of Scottish vermin", he said, "you will get nothing out of me" and he spat directly at McGregor who was nearest.

There was an awful silence. Red asked what the man had said, though its implications were obvious. To the left of us, a small band of dishevelled people were gathered, only one man among them he being badly wounded. A young girl approached Red, screaming in an hysterical voice, pointing her finger at the soldier now kneeling in the mud She accused him of killing her father, mother and baby brother, then of raping her, Big Red drew the girl into his arms, gently soothing her

Turning he said, "Take all of the women and children out of here"

But the young woman refused to go.

"Very well", said Red, "let her stay"

A quick command and the soldiers arms and legs were tied with leather thongs. They did not question him again.

"Hang him", said Red. This they did as he was carried screaming curses at them to the nearest tree. Colin approached another.

"Your name soldier?

A big hefty fellow who was sitting in the mud, "Go to hefl", he answered

The soft interpretation was given to Donald who grinned.

"You sir are a brave but evil man", saying this in soft highland Gaelic which the man could not understand. "Hang him"

Again this was done swiftly, as he joined his erstwhile friend on the tree. As his body swung gently in the breeze, another soldier was selected, this time it was a young man, possibly the youngest member of the troop. His name was Adam Sakene and had just graduated from drummer boy into an erstwhile trooper for Cumberland, and as such had tried very hard to prove himself to his fellow troopers, his raping and savage beatings handed out by him in an excessive desire to prove his manhood to others Now his courage deserted him as he pointed to a large portly figure whose eyes looked with hatred at the young lad.

"You cowardly rat", the officer spat at him, as he was dragged to his knees before Donald.

"Your name? Colin asked.

"Captain Clark Royal Dragoons"

"And your Commanding Officer?"

"Lord Gourge Sackville"

Red spoke to Colin without taking his eyes off the officer.

"He is unworthy to die as a soldier, he will die as a thief and a robber should"

This Colin related to the Officer, who merely spat out an oath, though his face took on a yellowish tinge.

"Let us see if you can die like a man", said Colin in English.

His hands tied behind him, he was taken to where the two figures still swung gently in the breeze. They stood him on a barrel. It was Big Red who kicked it away as he died screaming invectives at us. Red then gave a curt command to McGregor. The remaining prisoners were all lined up, then shot

"There is a swamp to the north of the Loch. We must remove every trace of them"

The bodes were packed onto horses and transported to the swamp, where weighted down with rocks, they disappeared forever. Red then set about removing all traces of the battle. They buried the ones in the village who had been killed by the troopers. Two of the McGregors band kith to the village, asked to stay and help comfort their cousins in this time of anguish. This was agreed and the rest of us moved out. I did not know the highland names for places, but I knew we were going in the direction of Braemar We camped the night in a large forest, and soon the fires were going. John and I sat beside Big Red as the assortment of highlanders showed each other their spoils, gold watchers, rings and jewelled daggers. The gold taken tonight would be evenly split by Red himself Later after supper was taken, which was a sheep, roasted on the fire, the money was shared out. Thirty eight gold sovereigns John and I each received. John grinned at me in the darkness.

CHAPTER SEVEN

Red called a war council and as we gathered around he drew a rough map on the ground, sketching where we were above Loch Lochy.

"We head from here across to Ben Adler. I want to talk to Cluny, he will have news of Lochiel. Then we turn north for Braemar, here we bury all the English trappings. We travel light"

There was a rumble of disapproval. A big black bearded highlander said, "I will not put a good harness into the ground"

A silence came over the group of men as each man was free to voice his own opinion, but even so, to go against the leader could cause death, Big Red rose to his full height. "Are ye deaf as well as dumb, man? Them harnesses creak and jingle and ye don't need the weight. Now sir, what's your name?"

"Lachlan Campbell, you bury yours first. I'm damned if I will", the big fellow said, "it's mine and I'm keeping it and if I have to leave to keep it, this I will do

"You may leave sir but you are not taking anything with you. If you are caught with that lot on you, they will torture you, till you confess"

"Is that so, well it belongs to me and 1 will take it with me"

As he said these words, the targe came from Big Red's back with his left hand his huge war axe in his right.

"Then you walk over my dead body sir,"

Lachlan dropped the harness saying, "You would kill your own Red Donald?

"Aye that I would", he replied, "though I have no taste for it", Donald said.

"Stay sir", said Red, "I want all of you to hear me. 1 am your Chief, McGregor is my second in command. Obey me, or leave now with nothing, or stay and fight and have your fill of English blood and plunder"

There was a chorus of "We will fight till we die", and a sheepish Lachlan extended his hand, which Red grabbed, then he put his arms around Lachlans shoulder and walked him to the fire. We had been moving across the mountains strung out in single file. The rain which had started early was now coming down in sheets the mist of clouds swirled around Us. When Red brought us to an abrupt halt without being told, the whole band melted into cover, of which there was plenty, heather, ferns and boulders. I crawled up to where Red was lying

"What is it" I asked.

"Shush", he said.

Just then eight men who were strung out appeared carrying out bundles. In a moment they were surrounded. They dropped what they were carrying drawing their swords Then one big fellow shouted, "Red Donald", and they rushed forward to grab hold of each other. Hearty greetings from the others as friends recognised friends. Tis the Glen Morriston Men, and as mixed a bunch of robbers as you are likely to meet. Rain or no rain, camp was set up on the spot. Quick rough shelters from cut birch branches with plaids draped over them. I found out that they were composed of mixed clans, one McMillan, two McDonalds, three Chisolms, one McGregor, one Grant and they lived off plundering the butcher's men, Once more after we had eaten, the whisky was ladled out generously.

"How did you know we were coming?" they asked. "Tis the dog Alistair, he cant bark but his teeth are very sharp"

With that they all laughed.

"He hates the redcoats as much as us", said Red. "Now lads any news?"

"Aye things are bad", said McMillan. "Lord Anchrim with the help of William McKenzie are burning every roman church and house, the Episcopals, are in the same boat. From here to Aberdeen, Cumberland has taken the leash off his dogs. They are confiscating all the cattle and horses, in fact everything they can get their hands on, murdering and raping their way through the Highlands. We wanted to kidnap Cumberland but Charlie would not allow it. God knows why, he is with Cluny in the cage at Ben Adler and is waiting on a boat to take him to France. Lord Gourge Sackville has taken 500 men from Fort Augustus to Glen Elq. They are killing everything in their path"

"Aye well they're 50 men short now", and they told them of what we had done.

"Is there anything we can do for you?" one of them asked.

"Would you care to join us?" Red asked.

"No thanks", they replied, "we have our own people to look after, We have a cave corredhugha in the braes of Glen Morriston, you are always welcome there. With that we wished them a safe journey and early the next morning we were off. As we were leaving Big Red eyed the quiver and bow very doubtfully.

"Tis no good to you Jamie, if you can't use it", at that he grinned.

"Oh I can use it Donald" Red answered with a grin, "We will see, tis no toy, and is a burden if it is of no use With that brief exchange, we were off.

There were hills, bogs and streams to be forded, Aye the kilt had many benefits, you just hiked up your kilt when fording any stream and in minutes your legs were dry, The rain continued to pour down as the silent file of men made their way across the mountains Skirting to the right, we crossed Rannoch Moor in driving rain, stopping only to eat oatcakes washed down with water. Night found us huddled miserably cursing the weather. We had camped in a huge overhanging rock formation. Every man set about building shelters of loose small boulders covered in ferns and peat, we did likewise.

Everyone was soaked to the skin, even so I just wrapped my plaid about me, then I was asleep, bone weary hungry beyond your imagination. As dawn light broke, it promised to be a fine day, The clouds broken, the sun peeping through, the sound of chopping as the huge war axes cut timber for the fires, which were soon blazing and the smell of porridge bubbling away, John sitting next to me having very little to say, since this adventure had begun.

"You're very quiet, John, you feel ok?"

"Im ok" he replied, looking at me, his now semi-bearded face gazed at me thoughtfully.

"How are you?"

"Oh Im fine", I replied

We were now conversing completely in highland Gaelic, as if it were our native tongue. He continued to speak very quietly, so much as I had to strain my ears to hear him,

"My conscience was bothering me at the beginning, but it does not now"

"How is that?", I asked.

"Well", says he "all these people are really dead anyway this is a time warp. Anyway Cumberlands men are butchers, so in a sense we must fight them when we are here Do you think we will meet Bonnie Prince Charlie?"

"Maybe", I said, "if he is still with Cluny"

"I am finding it difficult to remember my history"

I had barely stopped speaking when they started to fill the porridge bowls. Then a surprise, the big skin of whisky was ladled over the top of the porridge and they did not skimp the whisky. Lord I have never enjoyed such a lovely breakfast. Soon everyone was in a cheerful mood thanks Im sure to the generous amounts of whisky we had consumed. Filled with energy we broke camp and set off once more. The sun came out, warming us as we headed into the mountains region. Loch Eric stretched to my right as we started to climb. Once again the dog warned us of danger and we melted as one man into the rocks and vegetation. John and I stuck close together, soldiers or Jacobite. Then suddenly Big Red was on his feet. His huge face splitting wide with a smile, as around the bend, in the rocks a solitary figure stood His beard and dress made him look like a highland statue, then the undergrowth came alive with men shouting greetings at Donald and McGregors' men after all the exchanges of friendships had taken place, John and I felt out of all this, as we did not know anyone of them. It was the bow that caught the eye of McFerson, son of Cluny himself.

"Where did you get that?", he asked, Big Red told him briefly before I could reply

"Lets see if you can use it, James", said young Cluny.

We were on a flat piece of mountain ledge, which shelved for about 100 yards so I bid John whom knew I was fairly adept with the bow, to set up a target about 75 yards away. 1 had not tried it, now looking at it, I saw it was well made, good English yew. I adjusted the tension and selected an arrow. Meanwhile John had used his targe which hung on a small tree about four feet from the ground, the metal studs glinting in the sunlight. I wet my finger and held it up to feel the direction of the wind, then settled myself into a good stance calculating the flight angle. Apart from our first encounter with the enemy this was the only time they had paid us much attention.

"Steady as she blows", said John, his quiet words calming my nervousness.

"Aye aye sir", said I nonchalantly.

My first shot struck just at ground level of the target. Swiftly I placed another arrow on the string,

"Slight James, slight elevation" This time I struck gold almost dead centre.

There were shouts of delight from the crowd of men, and as there were 15 arrows left, they all wanted a go but they were not so successful. 1 retrieved all the arrows checking them carefully and returned them to the quiver.

"Where did you learn to shoot like that?", asked Red again.

The voice which was not mine spoke for me, "My father, Alistair Cameron taught me as did his father before him"

"And a fine job he did too", said Red,

"that was good shooting, you will come in very handy in the future lad, that you will"

"Now Cluny me lad, is Charlie with your father?"

"That he is" he replied, "and so is Lochief"

At that Red's eyes lit up, "Let's go then, we have no time to waste, I have much to say to him"

CHAPTER EIGHT

My heart pounded with excitement. Bonnie Prince Charlie, this to me, I don't know about John, but it was worth coming back in time. Cluny's cage as it was called, hung from the side of a cliff. A huge tree growing from the side of the cliff hid it completely as the cage was weaved through its branches, not a word was spoken as we approached.

"Stay here", said Cluny, "there is too many of you. I will ask the Prince if he will come and speak to you all Donald, you and McGregor come with me"

They left us and made their way into the cage. Twas about 20 minutes later, an old man dressed in faded tartan came towards them. Behind him a fairly young man very handsomely dressed in tartans. He smiled as he greeted us, asking as to our health. We all knelt on one knee but he bade us rise, then shook hands with each man, then touching his bonnet he bade us farewell and returned to the cage.

Red said, "I have spoken to Lochief, he is still unfit to travel but they have plenty of men here to look after him. We will rest here tonight and tomorrow we will leave for Braemar Red Donald and McGregor spent half the night in the cage, drinking and playing cards with the Prince, old Cluny, his son and Lochiel. Come time to leave, old Cluny had taken most of Big Reds money. I heard Red muttering about the old skinflint, as he bedded down for the night. The Prince, Cluny, his son and the rest of the men all waved farewell as we set off the next morning, fresh food and more whisky, it helped the long miles roll by. The light was fading when we made our first stop We had marched through the heat of the day and I felt pretty done in. Here at a small stream, we made our camp. Cold bannocks washed down with water, then a good bowl of whisky, Lord would I sleep. Just as we were settling down for the night, we were roused by the dog, warning us that a party was approaching us. Like wraiths in the gloom, we melted into hiding. Through the semi . . . darkness, we heard the clip clop of a pony and the ring of the wheels of a trap as it brushed through the heather, now and again hitting a protruding rock. Just then they came into view. An old man leading the pony by the head, two women walked beside him and something lay in the back of the cart.

"Hold there", said Red Donald. The women jumped in alarm, The old fellow let go of the pony, his hand flashing to his claymore.

"Don't alarm yourselves, we mean you no harm"

The woman looked about 50, the other 22. In the back, we found a boy of 12, badly wounded. The men grouped around as they told their story. The old man had been out cutting peat, when a party of Dragoons rode up to the croft. Her husband had been fencing off a piece of land by the side of the croft and they had surrounded him, nudging him with their horses, talking and laughing in their funny accents, Two women had run out of the house and the husband shouted for them to run. They knocked him down as he made a run for his pitchfork. One of them, who looked like their leader, walked his horse over him, then they put a rope around his legs tied this to the horses saddle and trailed him to a tree. They then strung him up, upside down.

Meanwhile the soldiers had surrounded the two women, As they dismounted, the women tried to run, their screams echoing across the valley as rough hands grabbed hold of them. Just then a boy ran into the yard from the house holding a sword. He made a frenzied lunge at one of the soldiers who deftly parried it, then ran his blade through the boy, catching him in the shoulder. As he dropped he laid his boot along the side of the boys head. He lay there in the mud as his mother and sister were brutally raped by 10 soldiers. The old man watch it all from a hilltop but realised he could do nothing to stop them, but give help when they had gone

Meanwhile, her poor husband had hung by the heels and watched In horror as they vented their filthy lust. One of them heard his screaming curses, drew his sword ran over to him and hacked his head off. He carried this over to his friends, who stuck it on a post facing his house which they then torched. The small amounts of cattle, they herded together. They had found a quantity of whisky in the house which they had looted. This they drank before setting off into the hills, leaving behind the body and the women lying in the mud of the yard, the headless corpse swung in the breeze as the old man came down to see what he could do. Some of the men were weeping when the old man had finished his story. John came forward, "Donald can I see the boy I know a bit about healing?"

"Aye that you can John"

Gently the boy was laid on the ground.

"Light a fire, boil me a pot of water", commanded John.

He reached into his war bag and pulled out a clean shirt which he tore into ribbons. The boy was still unconscious, as using his dirk, he cut away the boy's clothing to reveal a large stab wound just below the shoulder. He had lost a great deal of blood.

"Have any of you men any sewing needles and thread?"

"Aye I have", said an elder McGregor.

He spoke to his son, "Go get them out of my bag"

John washed the wound in hot water then poured whisky over the wound and dropped the needle and thread into the boiling water. Retrieving them, he sewed the boy up then turned to the boys face where a large gash split him from forehead to chin, this he stitched. When he had finished, the boy was wrapped in a blanket and placed on a bed of heather and ferns to make him as comfortable as possible. All this time the women had not said a word, seemingly ashamed of their humiliating violation.

"First the boy cannot be moved in that cart, it would kill him" He drew a sketch on the ground. "Two miles from here is old McHarg's cottage, It is high in the hills. I don't think the English will find it, so we take the boy and his people there, but we carry him" This we did, not stopping till we had climbed into a small box canyon where McHarg, a small bearded man with dark piercing eyes said he would look after the boy and those who were with him James said to John, "Give them our money", and as we did so, they saw the others doing the same. We camped the night there but before dawn we were off anxious to meet up with the miserable rats who had perpetrated this terrible atrocity.

CHAPTER NINE

It was the dog that alerted us just as we entered a large forest. Running back towards its master, who held up his hand, not one man moved a foot, just stood there in the gloom of the forest listening. We moved 200 yards as quiet as ghosts into the thick of the trees when we smelt the smoke from their fires. Now we were on our bellies as we crawled forward. Red held up his hand, we all froze. He then waved me forward. 1 slid up beside him peering through the undergrowth; There they were camped in a small clearing by the banks of the gurgling stream. To their right were about 8 head of cattle and 2 goats. One man walked the perimeter, obviously a guard. Only one tent had been erected and seated inside was the officer with two of his men. They were studying a map and in a deep discussion Seated around the two other fires were seven mean cleaning saddles, boots, swords and talking quietly. The whole scene so quiet, it was hard to think that these men had been such callous murderers, Red pointed to the guard then to my bow. I nodded to McGregor, He held up three fingers, pointed left, then three to the right and three to the back to cut off my retreat. 1 rose silently behind a large fir tree and fitted an arrow to my bow, then gently brought myself into view. As lined myself up to shoot, the guard was about 40 yards from the fire and had turned to make his way back. As he went through the motions of tedious guard duty, he had just slapped at a mosquito when my arrow caught him just below the throat. His hands flew to his head then he fell forward without a sound. 1 quickly fitted another arrow when I felt someone's eyes burning into me. It was my brother John. His deep thoughtful gaze, which he abruptly broke, as we waited for the signal to attack. The war cry of the Camerons rang out from Big Red, as with his war axe in his right hand, his targe in his left, he sprang at the foe. The English may have been brutal killers, but they were good soldiers, I paused with the bow lifted long enough to survey the battle area. Twas well

1 did, for as Donald closed with a large redcoat, another ran from the side of the tent, dropped to one knee with his musket aimed at Big Red, He saw him as he ran full tilt at the redcoat and knew there was nothing he could do but take one with him. His finger must have been curling on the trigger when my arrow caught him in the chest at the same time as Reds war axe almost cut his man in two. He paused there in the battle to wave his thanks, Meanwhile, John his shoulder laid open by a blow, killed a redcoat whose last act was to spit at John, cursing as he died,

Quick as it started, it was over. The officer was on his hands and knees, being badly wounded. Here the Scots showed no compassion. All were dead but for the officer and two soldiers. Strangely enough one was not even wounded.

"Your name, sir?" Colin said with a kick of his foot.

"Captain Teal"

"What company?"

"Dragoons under Lord George Sheville"

"Why had you only 10 men with you?"

"I was under Captain Clark's orders. He sent me out on a sweeping mission

"Where are you going?"

He gave no answer.

"It is enough", said Red Donald "make sure the rest are all dead. Hang these three"

This they did swiftly, eyes and mouth tightly bound as were their hands. The Highlanders did not like the dead or the dying looking at them, nor did they like a dying curse, hence the eye and mouth coverings. McGregor did something to the knot, for it took the officer a long time to die. Finally, it was over, the bodies all searched for loot and this time we had no casualties.

Though these men were killers. I found it hard to watch their execution. It was a nasty business, carried out in almost total silence by the rough highlanders only the struggling noises from the condemned.

"Remove all traces of them", said Red. The turf was cut and rolled back, long shallow graves were then dug and the bodies placed in them. After it was filled in, they replaced the turf, all excess peat was shovelled into the water of a fast flowing stream. When they had finished, you would not have known anyone was buried there. The tents and saddles went the same way. Soon all trace of them vanished. We moved on. The highlanders would not camp where they had killed, brave as they were. The fear of departed spirits and that they might return was strong in their mind. The wild mountain scenery was unsurpassed as we travailed in single file through the mountains We had in a short time become part of this strange highland group, now totally accepted as being one of them. They were a mottled variety, most having lost someone near or dear to them in this world. The only precious thing left to them was their pride and honour coupled with total allegiance to the Jacobite cause. I have heard big men cry for their lost dear ones, as they had one whisky too many, then in the morning light that same bright hard stare was back in place, the one thought vengeance, their own life was now as nothing. The lengthy stride of Big Red as he pushed us along, each one keeping up lest he become the subject of the swift banter of his kinsmen, We were very high in the mountains when the dog become excited.

Red slowed the pace and each man drew his claymore, Rounding a bend in the hills, we came on a encampment. Here a great number of people knelt in prayer. Alarm quickly spread through the crowd of women and children at our approach, but Donald calmed them with his quick smile. It was a French Jesuit Father Labone who was hiding in the hills to bring the mass and the sacraments to the people, He introduced himself. Red asked could we join in the service. He welcomed us. Afterwards the people shared their food with us, but Red was hungry for news. The priest told us of what was happening in the highlands, from one end to the other. Cumberlands' men were pillaging, burning, raping, their officers taking part with them, also demanding a larger share of the plunder. Many people being tortured before being put to death, to tell if they had any wealth hidden.

"God have mercy on them and us", said the priest, "the devil is running rampant through the highlands"

"Tis no way to live father, you can come with us"

But he refused, saying he would continue to work here with his people, knowing death would be the result of getting caught.

Red found out from the people that the soldiers had passed through here and had vented their hatred by killing 16 menfolk driving off their cattle.

"Where are they now?" Donald asked.

"They are all heading for Alvie, there must be 200 of them. We will get them", he promised.

He called a meeting with all his men, and told them of the proposed raid on the butchers men.

Pointing with the stick, he said, "Between Loch Eileen and Loch Ghamha is the old thieves road, called the Ratham Meirleach, I used to use driving the cattle over. It starts at Lochaber in the west and winds its way through Rothie Murenon along the south side of Loch Morlich and onto Loch An Uaine, the green loch and Ryvoan, We will go there first to the cave then we will see to the butchers men There was a general rumbling of discontent among the men.

"Yon place belongs to the little people", one big fellow commented.

"Aye it is", others chorused.

"Are ye men or children?", demanded big Red.

"Aye", said McGregor, "still your tongues. I have heard enough of this foolishness. Tis the little peoples' land that we don't deny, but we will leave food every day for them" and to this they all agreed. Over the fire that night, Red gave us his plan.

"Tis bold and dangerous", says he, "but if we do it right, small numbers though we are, we will get them all. First we will go to the cave with enough food and stores for the winter ahead, set up camp there, and at night we will go hunting the red devils. Put your fear of ghosts and such like out of your head, we have a job to do."

It was all agreed and in the morning we bade the Priest and the people farewell as we set off once more.

CHAPTER TEN

The mountains beauty fair took our breath away as the savageness of the boulder strewn country made you feel lost in its vastness, though John and I marvelled, the others paid no heed. To them it was commonplace having been born here, they took it all for granted The pace became much slower with many stops, as we were forced to skirt abandoned cottages which had their roofs burned off. Time after time, we had to stop to bury the dead, many of them women and children, I was sickened by the sight of so much horror, We came across people drifting aimlessly, no hope in their faces. Red took them with us and gradually our band increased till it now numbered 60. Odd men, women and children, our meagre supply of food was swiftly running out as we approached the green Loch. We had not stopped all day as our goal was almost within sight.

"My goodness John" I whispered, "look at that"

The light from the full moon shone down on the waters of the Loch and sure enough the water was bright green. We moved very silently as though in fear to wake the fairies. High above the Loch, Donald led us, when he suddenly held up his hand.

We appeared to be in a small boxed canyon, the walls towering on either side, growing from the sides of the cliffs, were a series of shrubs and bushes. Red ordered to gather brushwood to make torches.

"Do not light them out here", he commanded, "just follow me four of you, we will light the way for the rest"

Red waved John and I to his side, then reaching up he pulled the trees to one side and there before my eyes was a huge crack in the mountain wall, about 3 foot broad by 6 foot high, now I knew why Red had got rid of the horses

Before entering, Red spoke to the people who were now milling around the entrance.

"Sit down all of you", he said. He then asked two women for their shawls, These he draped over the outside to ensure that no light would be visible before he had lit their torches. The four of us entered the cave as the shawl was pulled back over the entrance. Red lit the torch.

"Good Lord", said John, "this is incredible"

The walls of the cave slopped downwards, then opened out to a huge gallery. In places the walls were very smooth, possibly the result of early volcanic action, as lava poured through here millions of years ago. Stalactites and stalagmites where shining like jewels in the torch light, like ghostly candelabra, the torch light unable to show us how high the roof was, Red placed the torches at the end of the cave and one by one, everyone filed into the cave. Everyone was very silent, their fear and uneasiness flowing through them.

"Don't be afraid, it's only a cave"

He then started to issue quick orders

"Light as many torches as we can"

Soon the whole place was lit up showing us a massive cave about 50 feet long by 30 broad. The roof seemed to go about 60 feet above our head and it was bone dry, Men came and went from the cavern gathering fuel for the fires Soon many fires were burning and the place took on a very different atmosphere. Red double sealed the entrance with woollen shawls, presenting two barriers to the light emitting from the entrance. The smoke rose from the fires to the roof, swirling as it did so, seemingly caught by some draught up there, then disappeared to the Lord knows where. Soon the air was filled with the smell of cooking porridge. It was a meal taken and enjoyed quickly as Red Donald said he would speak to us at the end of it, but first we pulled into the cave enough firewood to last for a month. One huge fire was then lit in the middle of the cave and we all made ourselves comfortable around it. Each man and women had a bowl of whisky in front of them, before Big Red started to speak. By his side, the bearded wild looking McGregor. Indeed as I looked around, John my own brother, tall, bearded, stained by war and travel looked as wild as any of them. Red was speaking again, interrupting my own thoughts.

"This is my plan. Tell me what you think of it. Starting tomorrow the fire wood you brought in, make sure that not even a twig is left, there must be no sign left that we were here. Tomorrow we wilt cut wood for shelters which we will build in here. We will cut the cave in half. Bring the heather for the floor and the beds, let nothing be dropped near here, neither twig nor leaf. When we have this place prepared, we will stock the cave with food. Have you any objections?" he asked. There were only murmurs of approval to this plan as Donald rose to his feet saying, "Let us sleep now. Tomorrow is going to be a busy day"

Dawn had hardly broken and we were up and about, Lookouts were posted at all the high vantage points. The rest of us set off into the heavy surrounding timber. Soon the cave took on a new look, like a small village, as a primitive lean to dwelling took shape, each man helping his or her companion. it was dusk before we were finished. There was enough firewood to see us through for many months ahead. Rather than half the place the men had built lean twos, the inside covered with dry heather, the entrance now had a wooden door which was camouflaged with peat and bracken, Red beckoned me over.

"Bring your bow James, you and I will go and get some fresh meat"

To McGregor he said, "Bring in the lookouts, we will not need them tonight"

To me he said, "Go get your brother"

McGregor called to one of his men to do as Red bid, then said, "I will come with you"

"Aye four of us will be enough" said Big Red, then we were off into the soft quiet beauty of the hills.

We had been travailing for about an hour crossing streams whose murmuring music 1 could listen to all day, their gurgling drowning out any noise we might make. Red held up his hand, we froze, He then beckoned me forward. Lord what a sight. A huge stag, its magnificent antlers giving it such a noble look as it paused for a moment, it's sixth sense working overtime. Luckily the wind was in our favour as very slowly 1 fitted an arrow to the bow. Hardly daring to breath I took aim. Its ears came up as if altered by the arrow or the twang of my bow, but it was too late, the arrow catching it in the neck. It turned to run then plunged to the ground, Red ran towards it, his dirk in his hand to cut the quivering animals throat, then turned to look at me with admiration.

"Laddie, laddie", he said, "that was a great shot"

Without more ado, he swung it up by the hind legs to a tree

"Leave it there to bleed", he said, "and we will go get another. Where there is one there is more"

Once more we set off, the towering mounts on either side with outcrops of huge boulders. It was John who saw it first, a young doe it must have dilly dallied too tong and had become separated from the herd, but there she was rubbing herself on a huge pine and nibbling at the bark. The range was a good 40 yards, and as before I did not miss, She crashed 20 yards from where she took my arrow, Again Red cut the animals throat and as he had done before, he hung it from a tree then quickly gutted it.

"Bury the waste", he said, "we were not here", with this he laughed. We made our way back to the other deer and did the same, burying the animals guts, trying to leave no sign we were there. Tomorrow the insects and animals will make sure there is nothing left So saying, he cut two poles and with these, we tied the legs of the deer and so carried them back to the cave. Soon the smell of roasting meat filled the cave and the praise was heaped onto my shoulders by Big Red for providing such a meal. The following morning the last touch was put to the cave, the entrance blocked off with one foot to spare by a huge door frame which was tied with heathery turn and a concealed small entrance to the right, which would open and shut to allow a large man with a burden to enter. So careful was their camouflage they ground small rocks to dust, this they scattered about freely, When they had finished you would not have known there was anything there. John grinned at me through a dirty black bearded face. Said he, "The mans a bloody genius If he had been the leader at Culloden, we would have won"

I laughed and agreed with him.

CHAPTER ELEVEN

That night Red called a counsel of war

"We will use ten men only to spy out the land. Each man is to carry a pistol, which you only use if cornered, With no chance of escape, kill yourself. It is not suicide, they will torture you to get information about the rest of us, it will save your own kith and kin. Are you all agreed?"

"Aye, aye", they all murmured. Strange as it was, John and I were willing to give up our lives for these people, yes people from the past yet we had become as one with them, enduring their hardship, feeling their pain, so from tomorrow our whole existence would be fraught with danger.

There was still plenty of work for those who were left behind, men chopping firewood as the women also helped them to weave the thin branches off the trees of the lean two cabins they had built. They knew the awful cold that sweeps across the highlands in the winters. At the far end of the cave they found a round hole about 5 feet wide, disappearing into the earth. Over this seemingly bottomless pit, they built two loos, one for men, the other for women. The children worked hard, walking up and down picking up bark twigs leaves which had fallen

Just as dusk was setting in we made our farewells. There were 10 of us, McGregor and 6 of his men. They all carried muskets except myself 1 carried my trusty bow but armed to the teeth, in my belt a flintlock, 1 hoped I would not have to use it on myself. Red Donald knew these mountains. He said he was heading for Alvie, but John and I were lost. The Gaelic names for places we had never heard, once said then forgotten, as no chord struck our memory, By mid-evening, we had passed two Lochs. There was no talk so we did not ask, not wanting to show our ignorance. We camped in a small well timbered valley and had a cold meal laced down with a bowl of whisky. I was getting right fond of the stuff, it washed down our oatcakes very well.

"You're well flushed laddie, you will be an alcoholic before you are finished" I just laughed but to be truthful I looked forward to my wee bowl each night.

"I think you might be right at that John", I said, "and your own self too eh", he just grinned but said nothing.

"Now", said Donald, "here we split up. Three to the south four to Alvie and three to the north. McGregor, myself and the two lads will head for Alvie, We will meet here after midnight. Without another word, we split up The others by mutual consent picked their own partners and once again we were off. We moved in single file through a dark stretch of forest, always on the alert for the slightest noise.

"it must be about 10 o'clock", I said to John

We were climbing out of the forest and the light was getting very dim, when we heard a noise approaching. We scattered into the deep heather and ferns and none too soon as a party of weary Redcoats came trudging through the hills. I took off my bonnet and slowly raised my head. They were following an old deer path, making no attempt to conceal their travel fifteen of them led by a small sergeant at arms. We listened as they vanished into the tall timber and we continued on our way. A half an hour later found us looking down an encampment in the semi-gloom, just outside Alvie.

A gallows had been erected in the centre of the small town, a mans body was swinging from it. To the right of the church, two houses were still smouldering. A woman screamed and a door burst open and a girl scarcely sixteen years old came running out, two soldiers following her. Fear lent her wings. She was stripped to the waist, her shirt hanging in ribbons as she ran. Glory be she is running this way. The girl was fairly sprinting up the hill to where they lay, the two soldiers following in full flight. Slowly they were cutting down their distance between them and her. One of them a big black bearded fellow let out a roar at her but by this time she was almost spent of energy

"Fifty more yards, lass", I heard Red mutter, twenty, ten, she fell almost five yards from where we lay. They came in fast now, the big fellow undoing the belt of his trousers as he came up to her still body lying gasping for air.

"You're mine lass, I will have you first, then I will teach you not to run again" It was his last words as Big Reds axe split the big soldiers head right down the middle. The other fellow tried to stop and turn but at the same time, my arrow caught him right in the throat. They both died without a sound.

Red said "Bring the bodies with us, we must hide them"

Gently he picked up the girl, stripped off his shirt and gave it to her.

"Quiet lass, you are going back with us"

We dug a shallow grave for them replacing the turf as we had done before, taking the girl back to the crest of the hill. We once again viewed the enemy.

"Whats your name girl?" asked Red.

"Eileen McDonald", she replied.

She started to thank us but Red placed his hand over her mouth, "Say no more lass, say no more. Now tell me how many people are left down there"

Eileen started to cry quietly, the tears pouring down her face.

"We were in church when they arrived. They came bursting in during the service. An officer fired his pistol at the roof and the minister came off the pulpit and told him that this was God's house and he and his soldiers must respect it. The officer then walked up to the minister, slapped his face saying not to speak to an English Officer in that tone of voice. The minister then told him what he thought of the English brutal killings"

"Indeed", said the Officer.

He then told two soldiers to take him outside and hang him. This they did. At the small gate tower they hung him, He never once pleaded for his life, saying only I forgive you, I only hope that God forgives you too, They just laughed and the soldiers kicked away the chair he was standing on. It took him some time to die as it was a bad knot, he choked to death very slowly. Twenty two men were then taken out of the congregation. These they shouted at screaming and asking questions brutalising them with clubs, whip and bayonet, One old fellow spat in the face of his tormentor who happened to be Captain Scott, of a supposedly good family. He went into a terrible rage and hacked the head off the old man, who died smiling Finally it was over and they were told to do a house to house search for weapons. This they did raping the women, young and old alike, stealing all they could get their hands on, rounding up all the livestock, they were showing no mercy.

"Now listen Eileen, is there any whisky down there hidden?"

"Yes", she replied, "but it is safe"

"Where?" says he.

"In the old barn at the bottom of the hill

"How much is buried there?" he queries.

"One hundred kegs", she replied.

"Indeed, indeed", said Big Red thoughtfully

I just sat watching her. She was a very lovely girl, long black hair, well built about 5 foot 6 tall, the large shirt tucked into a pleated skirt, pleated like a kilt of some dark material, She was gazing around her as Red asked her no more questions. Her eyes fell on me, then quickly moved away, but I swear I saw some interest in them, then it was gone, as Red said, "Let's get going, and as quickly we melted into the gloom once more.

At the meeting place we met up with the others who had returned just before us,

"No talk now", said Red, "we must get back, there is no time to lose"

By now darkness had settled in. Heavy clouds overhead threatened rain, as we moved as fast as we dared, without making a lot of noise. Lightning flickered overhead with the rumbling of thunder echoing across the mountains. I felt weak with hunger and fatigue, what with walking, climbing, wading through streams, yet not one person complained. Four hours later we were in the cave. The storm broke in all its summer fury, the lightning and thunder almost simultaneous in their togetherness. It was some storm and we missed out on it by so many minutes. John and I stood at the cave entrance watching the storm eating large lumps of venison, the blackness of the night lit up by the electric storm above. The rain was incredible.

"Boy we were lucky", John said, "let's go get some whisky"

We both grinned. "Aye, aye sir", James said and a half an hour later we were both fast asleep.

CHAPTER TWELVE

The morning dawned for us with the lovely smell of roasting beef, a whole deer skinned and roasting over the fire, two women constantly turning it as the fat dripped into the fire, The cave was very warm from the individual fires the clansmen burned. As many of them liked to keep themselves to themselves, but the food was shared out equally amongst us all the women doing all the cooking. The old men who had joined us had made themselves very useful scinning, keeping the fires going, bringing in water. Seen in the flickering light of the cave, it gave you a weird ghostly feeling not one person was idle, weapons cleaned plus sharpened, firewood constantly being chopped, sentries being changed and shelters being made more secure against the future winter cold. Both John and I spent most of the morning finishing cff our own sleeping quarters, when Red summoned everyone to a general meeting. As was usual we had just finished dinner and again the whisky was dished out. A quietness settled over the assembled people as Red held up his hand for silence.

"There are 150 soldiers at Alvie and they are well camped and armed. They are commanded by a Captain Scott, and McGregor says they are part of Captain Grants men. They will be waiting here to join him, and those treacherous dogs may have already put the people of Alvie to the sword, but I have a plan. Here, Eileen, come here"

The girl got up and approached the fire, Red put his hand on her shoulder as he told the people how she came to be with us. There were loud cheers as they heard how the two soldiers had died. Red praised me playing his own part down. I felt a deep sense of comradeship and no feelings of guilt at my own part in the slaying of the two men

"Now", said Red, "there are 100 kegs of whisky buried in the barn next to the church. Tonight four of us will take the girl into the town and she will find someone to tell the English where it is hidden, We will be in the hills above Alvie when they start to drink. At 3,00 a.m. we will strike. No one must escape. I want every English throat cut before two dawns have broke"

There was a silence when he had finished talking, then one young McGregor spoke up.

"I want to kill them as much as you Red Donald, but if we kill all of them, they will take their revenge by killing every man, woman and child within 100 miles

"Aye, you are right" said Red, "but we will hide the bodies. There will not a scrap of proof that they were ever here in Alvie when we are finished"

Again the silence, then Red said, "I want the Captain taken prisoner alive. I want to see the colour of his eyes when he dies"

At that, there was a loud cheer. Again Red held up his hand.

"Tonight when we leave, we take no food, each man a small skin of whisky. We will not eat till the job is done. Before you leave here, let each of you blacken your skin cover your weapons to stop them glinting in the moonlight Take nothing with you that jingles for tonight, we move like ghosts of the graveyard glens. Now, we have 50 men to their 150, yet 1 have no wish to cut a mans throat when he is sleeping, but it is another thing to take them by surprise, Attack them while they are sleeping off the drink We will split into two parties and when you hear my war cry, we will attack John James with McGregor will take care of the sentrys. Colin McDonald, here", he indicated to a tall highland warrior, "take four men with you and immobilise their four field pieces, stuff wet peat down the barrels. Callum Stuart, you take four men, get to their powder, when you hear the hoot of the owl, it will mean Colin has taken care of the field pieces. Have the fuses set, light them when you hear my war cry. Peter McFerson, take two men. Cut your way into the back of the Captains tent, knock him on the head, I want him alive. Are there any questions?" There were none,

"Go now see to weapons lads, prepare yourselves for there will be some of us who will not see the fight of day when this is over"

John and I sat close together at a small fire built just at the door to our small shelter. He was very quiet.

"A penny for your thoughts", I said.

He turned slowly looking at me thoughtfully.

"You don't seem to mind all this killing, how do you square this with your conscience? I hesitated a moment before replying. "1 must as a good Scotsman defend my country and its people in time of war, as we are now, in as much as if we had not joined this band and had wandered through the highlands aimlessly. We would have come across the rapings and killings, the savage butchery being meeting out to these people. What would we have done, stood and watched, taken notes, do nothing? Say well this is a time warp, they are all dead anyway, the English troops would have put us both to death, plus they would have tortured both of us. No John, as 1 live and too must die, I will do so as a man, and not as a mouse. I will fight for freedom against injustice and intolerance

"Whoa there", said John, holding up his hand and said with a large grin,

"Thank you James, you are right of course, you have cleared my mind of its cobwebs. I remember my history though I cannot say or think about it to Red Donald. It is as though my mind is blanked out"

"Mine too", I said, but he continued

"It comes easily to me when 1 just talk to you. I remember a letter that was sent by Hangman Hawley to a friend of his in London. In it he said, that if His Majesty would leave the foot infantry here and Parliament give the men a new pair of shoes for every rebels head brought in, I will undertake to clear this country. There are still so many houses to be burned and 1 hope many more to be put to death, though by computation, there is about 7,000 houses already burned, yet all is not yet done"

"I know, I know", 1 replied. "Hawley is an evil man, 1 too remember my history. The first thing he done when he arrived in Edinburgh was to build two gallows, one in the Grass Market, the other in the centre of Edinburgh"

Just then Big Red approached us. "Get ready lads", he said, "I want to be there before dark tonight"

As we prepared to leave, Red held up his hand, "Let there be as much silence in here as we can have. Now lads, let us kneel and ask God to guide us" This we all did, each person saying their own silent prayer, then were off trudging silently in the wake of Red Donald and McGregor. The girl stayed close by me and now and again I caught her looking at me with those big blue eyes of hers.

The sun was setting in a vast ball of orange fire over the mountains, the air after the storm was like sweet nectar from the Gods, the sky swept free from any clouds a deep blue promising a clear starlit night. There was as usual no small talk just the long limbering stride of the highlanders, the girl having no trouble keeping up with us, she being born and bred to these mountains Now and again we would stop as Red and McGregor would scout forward, then once again we would be moving. The stops became more frequent as we approached Alvie, Soon as in the night before we lay atop the hill looking down on the small settlement To the north of the town neat rows of tents, where occasionally we could see soldiers moving about, the body of the minister was still hanging to the left of the church now a burned out ruin East of the church, four more bodies hung from a tree. Dusk was settling in quickly as Red crawled back to where the girl lay between John and I, saying, "I will come with you lass" As he grasped her arm, "No Donald", I said, "let me go, I am smaller than you, they would spot you a mile away" He grinned softly in the darkness.

"You are a good man James, and a brave one. Here take my pistol. If you are trapped, kill the girl then yourself.

"Have no fear. I will do what you say, they will get no information from the dead

He shook my hand saying, "Come back safe lad", as the girl and I slipped slowly down the hill.

We moved like wraiths through the mist that was rising from the valley floor.

"The house on the left belongs to Gordon McDonald the blacksmith, he must be 80 years old", Eileen whispered in my ear. She came very close to me as she spoke and I felt her hot breath in my ear. I turned to speak to her before she had finished talking and so quickly did I move that my mouth accidentally brushed hers. Heavens she was beautiful. We both froze for that moment in eternity, the war was forgotten. She being so close to me, our sensual awareness sharpened, as our eyes locked on one another. Then my arms were sliding around her and our lips met once more.

She pushed me away saying, "James, James, we have work to do", then she smiled saying, "there will be time soon", so saying she threw her shawl back over her head and we crept up to the old mans cottage. The door was ajar as with a gentle push we were inside. Lord the place was wrecked, furniture smashed, floor boards ripped up, anything of value taken. The old man lay in the comer of the room. I turned him over gently, his face had taken quite a beating. He moaned quickly. I said, "Get some water"

I took a small flask of whisky from my pouch and gently lifted his head, wetting his mouth with the alcohol He groaned again as he opened his eyes,

"Here Gordon, drink a little water"

He took a little as I gave it to him, a sip at a time. I wet a piece of cloth and wiped the blood off his face.

"Eileen set one of those chairs up", and between the two of us, we got him into the chair. I then gave him a good snort of whisky which indeed revived the old fellow.

"You will be alright now", I said, "no ribs broken"

"Who are you son?" he asked enquiringly. I told him who 1 was, then asked is the whisky still safe.

"Aye", he said, "why do you ask?"

I said, "We must give them the whisky. We want them all drunk by tomorrow night, it is important so we need someone to tell them where it is, question is who?"

"There is only one person who would tell them and the wee soul knows neither right nor wrong, just tries to please everyone"

"Tis Alistair you are talking about", Eileen said quietly. "He has only a childs brain so the townsfolk tell him nothing because he cannot keep a secret"

"Where is he just now?" I asked, "oh he will be down at Mary Grants house, she has a place for him in the cellar"

"Then we must get him", I said, "there is no time to lose"

"Leave", said the old man, "I will be alright"

"You will be that I promise Mr McDonald in a short time"

With that we were off, keeping to the shadows. Eileen guided us to Mary's house Again the door was half open and we found old Mary sitting in an old rocking chair weeping quietly. She was about 70 years old, small white headed lady. When we entered and she recognised the girl, she wept bitter tears. As the girl held her in her arms, she told us the soldiers had ransacked her house, slapped her about and took everything, the things her father and his father had before him.

"Look", she said rolling up her sleeve, her arm was black and blue. "They laughed and cursed at me. One of them, a big fellow hit me on the arm with his musket butt, knocking me against the wall. My head took a bang and when I came too, they were gone"

"You shal't have it all back Mary, this I promise you", I said, "but you must do something for me"

"What is it? she asked.

"Go tell Alistair where the whiskey is kept. Say to him not to tell the soldiers

"But", said Mary, "it is the first thing he will do, God help him, he has no sense

"I know, I know Mary, just say to him"

"It is a good job they did not find the whisky that's hidden in the old barns floor Next to the church, that is what he will tell the Redcoats, he is brainless, but a little fly as well"

"Now Mary mention to him how some person could be rewarded for that information

"I will do it lad, now be off with you before they come back" Eileen kissed the old lady and we slipped outside into the gathering darkness. We slowly made our way back to where the others waited. Quickly I related what we had done to Red Donald and showed him a drawing I had made of the enemy camp, The night was clear, our way lit by the stars and it seemed no time at all we were back at the cave, Within 5 minutes we were asleep.

CHAPTER THIRTEEN

Dawn found us once more in an after breakfast war council. Again we related what had taken place. Red produced my drawing of the enemy camp and once again he outlined the attack procedure. So it was, we would leave after dark, Red wanted us on the hill ridge at midnight Each man knew his job.

"Any questions", said Red. There was none.

"Then lads may the fairies of the glen bring us luck"

Twas a strange thing for him to say but over the last two days the talk in the cave was of the strange happenings on the green Loch. One young lad said he had seen the water cut in half by a red swath, others, that hundreds of small lights had appeared on the water itself At first, he had thought it was the Redcoats but nothing appeared to come out of the water Long as he waited and watched by the fires in the darkness of the cave the talk often ranged about the little people. The Braham Seer who after sleeping on a fairy hill awoke to find his head on a small stone with a hole in it. He tried to look through the hole with his right eye which was then blind to everything except truth and the future, but the man they all feared the most was Patrick King of all the Leprechauns. Each had a story to tell always someone belonging to them had seen the fairy these beautiful Gaelic people, unafraid of death yet afraid of the fairy folk. It was hard to understand, they even mentioned Thomas the Rhymer whom they said fled to fairyland. This John and I knew to be true but could not speak a word

Not a day had passed since we had arrived that the highlanders did not put food and drink at a giant chimney rock for the little people and so help me it was gone the next morning. The talk grew less and less around the fires as the time approached. Clansmen fussing over weapons sharpened to razor point faces legs, hands, blackened they were indeed a wild looking bunch, John his beard matted with soot greeted me with a grin.

"Man" he said "'you look like Blackboard the Pirate"

I quickly retorted "Look whos talking, you look like something the cat brought in" We both laughed.

It was getting dark as Red Donald assembled his troops, The old men and women were told to have food ready for us on our return, then in one swift motion he drew his claymore, raised it above his head, knelt down and kissed the blade once more brandished it shouting "For God and Charlie" A roar went up filling the cave with noise, as each man there echoed him. I felt my heart bursting with the fires of Scottish passion, then once again the silence.

"May God guide our hand", shouted Red Donald, then we were off. Once again the eerie silence as 50 warriors moved as silently as the Apache Indian, We had no trouble reaching our position overlooking the town and as we watched, soldiers were singing and dancing around their fires. We could make out a huge pile of kegs next to the officers main tent. The time must have been near midnight and the soldiers were in a good party mood. We watched as a soldier walked shakily over to one of the sentrys, handing him a bowl of whisky, which he quickly downed. We counted 5 sentrys. The Captain came out of his tent and urinated, then went back inside. Before 2a.m. the camp lit by a full moon was growing very quiet, only sporadic singing. Three sentrys were dozing, two stood by the fire drinking another 10 minute silence descended over the camp. Red signalled to McGregor. Four men slipped forward, dirks between their teeth, They got within 10 yards of the two sentrys by the fire. They palmed their dirks and threw them with deadly accuracy. The two men died without a sound. They quickly pulled the bodies into the darkness and recovered their weapons. The other three sleeping sentry& did not feel the blades cutting their throats. Red waved his hand again, Four men to the field pieces, their barrels to be filled with peat, two men slid off to the powder tent, two to the Captains tent. Again we waited. Red whispered, "Get your bow ready James, tie the arrow with straw, when you hear the owl hoot three times, light it and send it down into the nearest tent" I quickly tied up an arrow and waited, John with the flint, then we heard the hoot of the owl. On the first John was sparking the flint, on the second it was igniting and on the third it was in flames. I fired high. It arched skyward and fell direct into the first tent. Just then the powder tent blew up and all hell broke loose. Soldiers came stumbling out of their tents, some armed with small broad swords, only to be cut down by the savage highlanders pistol shots. Screams of the dying, curses of the living and John and I were in the thick of it. We moved forward, hacking, thrusting our blades running red with blood. A large bearded giant of a man, one of his braces hanging down from his trousers, he had just killed one of the McGregors and was pulling his blade free, it came up in a wild swing just missing me, then my blade took him through the throat. A look of surprise, then horror, a shudder then he fell. Quickly I looked for John, I seen two men coming at him. I yelled to John, we fairly flew to each other's side, They were no match for our blades and died quickly. An officer stood, two pistols spurting flames and another of our men fell mortally wounded. Before he could reload, I ran him through, back to back, side by side, we found sweeping the Redcoats before us. Two of the field pieces blew up killing the soldiers, the smell of blood was everywhere, The soldiers were now trying to run, no one to lead them. They did not know that we were outnumbered, it became a slaughter house. As they threw down their weapons and tried to run to freedom, but only into the jaws of death, so completely were they ringed, not one man escaped out of 150 soldiers, only four had survived, not counting the Captain. Red's men walked among the fallen seeking any wounded. They found 12 more, they carried them to the side, then Red gave the order.

"Make sure the dead are dead", and believe me, this they did Red secured his prisoners and we combed the area for miles around to make sure no one had slipped through our fingers. Two were found in the town, both young officers, still very drunk, one of them could hardly stand up.

CHAPTER FOURTEEN

The dawn light was breaking as Red Donald prepared for his court-martialling of the prisoners. He sent Callum Stewart to find Mary. "She must keep the boy locked up. He must not know of anything that has happened here today. Light a large fire"

This they did, then the first officer was brought over, his hands tied behind his back. It was the one who was very drunk.

"Your name sir?' said Colin.

The officer did not reply Colin poked him with his sword.

"Lt Brown", he said his voice slurred with drink, "how many did you have?"

No answer. Red asked what he said. Colin replied, "He will only give his name"

Donald put his dirk into the fire and we all waited in silence. The young officer vomited onto the ground as he swayed unsteadily on his feet.

Colin looked at Red and he nodded his head.

Again Colin asked "How many men have you, do not lie"

The Officer straightened himself up, vomit running down his beardless chin onto his open jacket and vest. Still he did not answer Red gave a curt command. Four men pinned the man to the ground and Red drew the dirk from the fire, the Officer kicking and struggling to no avail. As Red approached him, one sharp tug and the mans vest was ripped from his body.

"Ask him again", said Red, as he stood over him, the red hot dirk inches from his belly

"150", the man screamed.

"Ask him if command knows they are here"

He shook his head violently "The Captain took a fancy to come this way"

Red signalled to drop him, he lay quivering on the ground. Once more Red placed the dirk on the fire, "Gag him, now we will see if he tells the truth"

They brought out the second officer.

"Your name?", said Colin.

"Lt Grey, how many men had you?"

The man looked about him. He was a fat portly figure of a man, small pig eyes gleaming through the folds of flesh on his face.

"500", says he swiftly sweat beading on his brow"

"You lie sir, there was 150. Where are all the rest?"

"They are due back today", the man replied. "You will all pay well for this days work"

Colin relayed what he had said. Again Red motioned with his hand. Once more they pinned their man to the ground. Red drew the red hot dagger from the fire.

He said to Colin, "Tell him he is a liar, remove his boots"

Cursing and screaming, the man shouted. "I am telling the truth"

The man let out an unearthly scream as Red applied the dagger to the sole of his foot. The officer was screaming and writhing about in agony. The smoke was still rising from his foot as Ted said ask him again.

"150", the officer said, his very words choked in his agony.

"Does anyone know you are here?"

"Yes command does

Again the blade rested on the mans foot. "No, no", he screamed.

"Take him away. Bring the Captain"

Again the blade was placed in the fire. The Captain was brought out. He was an arrogant looking fellow, tall with a large belly, gazed at us arrogantly. Colin asked,

"Are you in command here?"

The officer spat on the ground saying, "Tell him I am an English gentleman and refuse to answer any of his questions, You vermin are beneath my contempt"

Once again he spat on the ground Red Donald growled, "Ask once more"

This he did.

"Go to hell", the Captain said.

"Tie him to that post and strip him to the waist. Your name?", said Red in Gaelic as he waved the red hot dagger beneath his chin, The Officer spat at Big Red who merely placed the flat of the blade on the man's belly. He screamed then his head rolled forward unconscious. They threw water around him and he came too writhing in agony.

"Your name?", said Colin.

"Captain Scott, how many men have you?"

"500", he said. Again the red hot blade, he screamed but did not faint this time, just babbled, "150, 150"

"Does anyone know you are here?" asked Big Red.

"No, no", he babbled, "No one"

Red brought out the other prisoners They were all brought forward, some wounded from battle, 18 in all. Red held up his hand and said, "We find you all guilty of murder and rape, as such you are no longer soldiers but killer dogs, I sentence all of you to death. The three officers will hang, the rest of you will be shot"

One by one, the three officers were hanged, Captain Scott was last of all. He was crying as they led him to the scaffold, the rest of the soldiers were shot. Most of them died like men, some hurling their defiance at us as they were shot. Finally silence reigned on that scene of utter carnage, we had lost only 7 men and victory had been complete.

Red Donald gathered his battle weary men around a large bonfire. My Lord, I got so close to the flames I almost burned, so cold was I, The villagers or what was left of them gathered with us, as Donald outlined what we would do with the dead. "We will bury them beneath the church they destroyed, let the Lord guard their bodies from our enemies. If word goes out what we have done, many Scots will die. We will bury them beneath the cobble stone floor, maybe when we have peace, we will rebuild the church there again"

All through that long wearisome day, we performed the gruesome task of burying the dead soldiers, the highlanders having no scruples in stripping everything from the dead Every corpse was naked as it was dragged to the huge hole that we had dug. Beneath the floor of the church, every piece of weaponry was taken by the Scots and finally it was over as the last cobble stone was put back in place and Red Donald gathered us all together and we knelt in prayer, as he asked God to please look kindly on what we had done and to spare the innocent if we were found out. After concluding the small ceremony, Red Donald bade us scour around for the slightest piece of English equipment, or whatever When not a trace was left of the regiment we sat down to eat, it being about midday and the whisky was passed about quite freely. Soon John and myself were in very good spirits. When we had eaten we set out restoring the roofs of the houses, removing all traces of the church, except the floor. As we prepared to leave, I took a last look back and it was hard to believe that sleepy looking hamlet I was now looking at had such a short time ago been the source of so much blood letting and horror.

I went looking for Eileen and we sort of found each other as it were I felt a strong pull towards this remarkable girl and as she approached me I had the strangest feeling we would somehow take her back with us. Before I could think anymore, she was in my arms, her long beautiful hair cascading over us both

"Oh Jamie", she said, "I feel as if I have known you forever"

I kissed her and from that moment I knew I was in love As I held her close, my mind was racing ahead. I won't let her go, I won't.

"Take me with you Jamie", she was saying.

My Lord, how could I. Here I was a stranger from another time. Even if we could, would she like it, when there is no going back. I looked deep into her lovely eyes, as she again said, "Jamie take me with you, I have no one left", and in that moment I know that no matter what, we would be together always

"Eileen", I said, "come sit down over here"

As I sat her on an old tree stump and said, "I love you Eileen" she said, "I love you too James"

"But you don't know me", I said.

She smiled warmly, "I know all I need to know"

I looked at her as she sat there looking so very alone. What if I could not get her back to my own time, was I prepared to stay and I knew without any further thought, I was and would if necessary. God knows what John would think of all this. She was watching my face and seemed to know even before I had said it. I grinned and said, "What the hell, let's go"

CHAPTER FIFTEEN

The journey back to the cave seemed to take forever, yet for me it was not long enough as I got better acquainted with this very lovely girl. She told me how her family had been wiped out by the soldiers. She had been up in the high pastures with their cows when they had raided the farm,

She had returned to find them all dead, father, mother and two brothers. For the past month she had lived alone. She had entered the village the day before the battle, not knowing it was occupied with troops. That's when they had found her. When she tried to ask me questions about myself, I was vague in my replies. The return did indeed take longer as we were burdened down with a great deal of booty, plus food, guns and ammunition. The gunpowder kegs we strapped to two donkeys we got from the village, the field pieces we sank in the bog. The moon was scudding in and out of the clouds as we finally arrived at the cave. The old men and women we had left behind had the fires going and food prepared for us coming back. Lord I was so tired I could hardly speak. I was not the only one for there was little talk as we ate. I gave my plaid to Eileen, while I once again shared with my brother. We all three bedded down in a small lean too we had built, then we slept the sleep of the dead.

We awakened to the lovely smell of roast beef and yes you've guessed it, porridge After eating, we gathered around Red Donalds fire. Here all the gold sovereigns taken were divided equally, there were 3,000 in all. Along with rings, broaches bracelets, a silver walking stick, saddles, silver, dirks, jewelled handled swords, obviously ceremonial swords, even a silver horseshoe, everyone wanted this for luck. Big Red held up his hand, "I say give this to the little people, along with 200 gold sovereigns"

There was a silence, then everyone agreed. So it was arranged. James and I were elected to go out at midnight and place the gold and silver horseshoe at the fairy stone. At the entrance to the land of bold King Patrick, Eileen stepped forward, "May I go with them?" she asked.

At this request, Big Red laughed, "Already she won't let you out of her sight", and he agreed.

I looked at John who seemed to be somewhat haggard looking but still looking every inch the noble Scottish warrior he was. I said to him,

"I have much to talk to you about John, and it concerns the girl"

He looked at me questioningly. "I love her John and I will not be parted from her

"Steady now old son, steady", said John, "do you know what you are saying. How can you say you love this girl when in fact you have only known her for a few days"

"I know, to" you John, it looks like a quick infatuation, but is not, quite simply, I love her so much I would die for her"

John shook his head, "You are under a great strain, what with all this happening, you don't know your own mind. Have you told the girl?"

"I tried", 1 said, "but as per usual I could not get a word out"

"What happens if they will not let you take her with you?"

"Then I shall stay here John and we must go our separate ways"

John stood and looked at me for a few moments without saying anything and as he turned he said, "We will leave it in the hands of God"

The highland people are a very astute bunch, they had been watching us from a small distance and had sensed our disquiet, but thinking it was fear for the girl's safety, they wanted to set our fears at rest saying, "Don't be afraid of them, they will not harm you or the girl, just find out if this is enough gold for them, if not we will give them more. I took one last look around this dark cavern, noting the strange wariness of these highland people who were so afraid of the Leprechauns.

I gripped Red Donald's hand and said, "Take good care of yourself Red Donald" for John and I knew we might not be coming back.

"Aye that I will lad and you too, beware of them fairy folk, they have terrible powers, Tell them we will winter here and be off when the trouble is over"

CHAPTER SIXTEEN

John, Eileen and I made our way out into a clear moonlit night, the stars arrayed in their millions. As the trees started to thin out into what looked like a blind canyon, it was as they had described it There before us was the fairy table, as if it had been carved out of the stony mountain itself, here where for countless number of years, the mountain people had left their tribute to the little people, but tonight as we made our way over to the table like rock, the very air seemed to be alive with tension. The whole valley was lit up by the light of the full moon. Eager to be off from this ghostly place we laid on the rock the peoples tributes, the 200 gold sovereigns and the silver horseshoe.

As we turned to go, John gripped my arm very tightly.

"What in heavens name is that?", he said, for the valley was suddenly almost obscured by waves of rolling mist, but they were all the colours of the rainbow. I grabbed hold of Eileens hand saying, "Come on John, lets get out of here", but my feet were frozen to the ground.

"I can't move", John said in a faltering voice.

"Nor l", said Eileen.

"Try, try", I said, but I too was stuck fast.

By some unearthly power, I felt the hair rising on the back of my neck as the mists swept back revealing the sheer cliff rock face, then before my very eyes, the rock started to open wider and wider, light as bright as the sun bursting forth to reveal inside the mountain a beautiful palace shimmering as if it was made from gold. Hundreds of little people dressed in green tunics with feathers in their pointed caps walked on either side of a small chariot drawn by the smallest horses they had ever seen. Slowly they approached the table where they stopped. Two small figures opened the carriage doors, a small lady emerged, then another figure dressed in the regalia of a King. A green cloak covered in stars with gold thread, he looked to us like one of those latter day picture book Kings. So colourful was he, on his head was circled a gold crown, his face had a large white beard. He paused to speak briefly to the lady beside him before approaching the boys. He came within 10 yards of them before stopping. We waved his hand, whereupon a figure dressed in the finest tunic, weaved with gold, approached them and said,

"His Majesty King Patrick and his wife Queen Martha wishes you welcome and desires to speak with all of you" Then in a low voice he said "Go forward, kneel, pay homage" With that, he turned walked back and resumed his place behind the King. We walked slowly forward and about 5 yards from the royal party we knelt on one knee. Your Most Gracious Majesty, he was indeed an old, small bearded figure. His wife herself though showing her years, looked very dignified. The King waived his hand saying,

"Arise young Sirs and you too my fine lady. You have come far in time and place, I bid you welcome, short though your stay in my lands. So you are the young men Thomas brought back here. We have watched you both, have we not Martha?

"We have indeed Patrick", she said, smiling her face lighting up, showing an inner hidden beauty.

"How are you young lady?" she enquired. "You will be Eileen the young women who has fallen in love with James?"

Eileen curtsied and said "Yes Your Majesty but I do not understand what is going on. Who is Thomas?"

"All in good time young lady", the Queen said. "Look to your left young sirs, tell me what you see"

We looked and there was nothing but rocks and trees, They laughed.

"Look again my friends"

Lo and behold, standing there dressed as he was before was Thomas the Rhymer. He bowed to them.

"Your guardian I believe", chortled the King. With that hundreds of little people who had been gathering, laughed.

"You have done well", said the King, "but it is time to return from whence you came

"But", I said, "what of Red Donald and his band of men, what will become of them, he needs us"

A look passed from the King to Thomas. "Your heart is heavy, it is but a passing acquaintance"

"No", I said, "I speak for us all. He needs all of your help and ours"

"Tis full of kindness that you are young sirs, but being what it may, you must return to your own century"

"Your Majesty", I said, "I have fallen madly in love with this young lady and would have her return with us"

On those words there was a brief silence as the King eyed both of us speculatively then he whispered something to his wife who smiled and inclined her head. He turned back to us once more saying, "And so it shall be but the gift I give here is she will be able at all times to return if perhaps she is unhappy"

We both thanked him profusely. Three small men approached us carrying small cushions in their hands. "Here is a parting gift I give you", and there on each cushion was golden rings. They stopped before the King, bowed, and he then presented them to the boys and the girl. The King said, "Whatever your trouble, no matter what it be, rub on those magic rings, you will be summoned to me"

John who till this moment had remained very silent said quietly, "We thank Your Majesty but what of Red Donald and our friends?"

The King beckoned Thomas the Rhymer forward saying, "Explain to them Thomas the value of time Thomas stepped forward and said, "Time my friends to us means nothing as you now stand between two worlds, time has leapt forward, time is for mortals. You were as you know taken back, back so you could tell the people of your time, what my people suffered. You have stood up to this very well and my King and the people of this land are very pleased with you. The girl, you may speak to her of the future because she must understand where she is going

He bowed to James saying, "You must do so now"

Bowing once more he walked to his place behind the King.

"Would you please excuse me Your Majesty?" I said. He nodded in assent.

I took Eileen by her two hands and said, "I sincerely love you Eileen but I have something to tell you"

She was gazing at me, her eyes full of fear and tension

"What is it James?" she queried.

She looked so lovely, standing there in those faded tartans, her long hair cascading down onto her shoulders. I kissed her and said, "I am from the future"

"I don't know what you mean", she said

"Well this is 1747, I am from 1996 and I must go back and I want to take you with me. Will you marry me sweetheart?"

She was crying now as she wrapped her arms around me and said, "Oh yes, oh yes"

I called to John. "I am getting married"

He grinned hugely and gave us both a hug. "I hope you will be very happy", he said

Once more Thomas came forward. "You have asked about your friends and the King has said you should be told" so saying Thomas waved his hand the crowd parted and there before my very eyes was a small figure dressed in highland regalia who started to grow before our very eyes to a veritable giant,

"Red Donald", I shouted.

He grinned hugely, "Aye lads, they took us all in that bad winter of 47. Look lads", sprouting like giants they popped up one after the other all cheering us. His massive arms circled us.

"Tell them boys, tell them what you have seen and done, tell them to be proud of the brave highlanders"

He shook hands with all three of us bowed to the King and the Queen then started to shrink back to the same size as the rest of the little people. Even their clothing changed to a dark shade of green. They all cheered as the King said, "Till we meet again"

Thomas stepped forward and said,

> *Those rings are now your own rings, and will hold you in their clasp, as I release the magic, all things will come to pass, the knowledge that it gives you, will never fade away, the power of all eternal, will take you home today*

Whereupon he waved his hand and once again we were tumbling into a vortex of a whirling whirlpool, the blackness being replaced by a blinding light. We came too, the strong sunlight burning our eyes, lying on our backs on a Scottish hillside overlooking Anchinnary Castle. We sat up and look dazedly at one another, our lovely tartan trews soaked in sweat. We both looked at one another, my Lord, surely not a dream?

Just then a voice filled with terror. "James James", as Eileen topped the hill and ran into my arms.

The End

CULLODENS LAMENT

Through the fields of blood soaked Culloden, 5,000 men they came,

to fight for Bomlie Charlie, aye their freedom for to gain,

against them stood 9,000 troops, as Cumberland took his stand,

then routed Bomlie Charlie's men, that day we lost Scotland,

2,000 Scots died on the field, the rest fled in disarray,

that did not stop the butcher, he slew them on their way,

he burned and raped my Scotland, pillaged church and town,

the Jacobite Rebellion, he swore to put it down,

his soldiers now were killer dogs, the butcher let them loose,

as they slacked their thirst with Scottish blood, now the butchers vital juice,

from the highlander he took their land, with no place to call their home,

as they died yes in their thousands, no food no roof no home,

ah yes the Scots lament their kin folk, who died that April day,

but the ones they had left behind, had a terrible price to pay,

now as the moon rose ore Culloden, I walked on that hallowed land,

when a figure appeared in the moonlight, a Jacobite claymore in hand,

kilted gaunt and so weary, he looked into my frightened eyes,

go tell the people of Scotland, twas for freedom that at Culloden we died.

THE LEPRECHAUNS

Dunlavy village nestled quietly in the countryside of Galway peace and poverty came together in this the time of our Lord 1897 the little houses huddled together bonding the community the church the pub being the two central places of worship it also had a blacksmith, a hardware come-by-anything shop, a barbers and a school. Poor yet in a way for that part of Ireland prosperous. The outlying farms and small holdings and the big house owned by a virulent old lady called Mrs Jenson who with its many extensions she had built, tried to make the large house called Waterside look like a small castle. The village supplied the servants and the labour for the two farms that they owned, the stable held a good string of horses used by the many guests who came to the house.

Casey O'Rourdan the farm manager was a large robust man going bald he always dressed in tweeds as if he was a retired Englishman, he was indeed a hard task master extracting every ounce out of all the men who worked for him. Today he had just purchased for the old lady another small farm which had belonged to a man named Branigan. His one daughter lived in England and she was married to a doctor and did not want to return to the old country, unbeknown to her, the old man had given 5 acres of his land to a man called Seamus O'Toole. He was known to all the people in the district as a man to keep friends with as he had—they said—the gift, he was the seventh son of a seventh son and one of these gifts was the curing of anyone with the worms, cattle included. He was called on many times to perform his small works of magic, the seven cures gained him a great deal of respect in the village and surrounding area but to say the least the wee man was in a state of shock.

He and Branigan had been lifelong friends; he never thought to sign the land over to him or indeed put it in his will which was anyway non-existent. Now it was to be absorbed by the Jensen's small empire. Branigan had scarce been in the ground eight weeks when the daughter sold out to the Jensen's and now September when the fruits of 0'Tooles labour were about to be Harvested 0'Rourdan with his large beefy face, his big whisky nose told 0'Toole he must get himself off the land forthwith. 0'Toole nearly had a stroke he was of small stature and about 64 years old he still had all his hair which was almost pure white thin and wiry he ranted and rated at the farm manager

"ye sir can't and won't do this to me daid and an ye won't" he ranted

"that sir we will the law will be on ye iffin ye don't git off now" Says 0'Rourdan

"what about me crops?" O'Toole quizzed

"what about them?, they're ours now that's jist to bad" said 0'Rourdan with a sleekit sneer and saying so walked away leaving a flabbergasted 0'Toole.

On arriving home he told his wife Nessie she knowing his temper tried to calm him down

"go see Mrs Jenson she won't know the circumstances" she said

"oh bejabers" said Seamus "she's a miserable oul witch shore she'll set the dogs on me" but out of desperation he put on his Sunday suit and off he went to the big house pedalling slowly on his old bike. The estate pathway lined with Poplars and Rhododendrons, a small lake dropped off to his right completing the beauty of the whole area. Seamus left his bike at the servants entrance and made his way up to the large oak door a large skull head knocker adorned the door.

Boom Boom he could almost hear the echo the door was opened by the butler, a large beefy man who's tight suit seemed to have reached its maximum expansion

"yes"

he said in an impeccable English voice

"I would like to speak to Mrs Jenson"

"and whom may I ask are you" he replied

"Seamus 0'Toole to be shure"

"wait here" he said closing the door in his face. It seemed like an eternity but in fact it was about ten minutes, the door was swung open again by the Butler

"come this way" he said

Seamus removed his bonnet and followed him down a long passageway, the walls lined with portraits. He stopped at a large door, knocked gently before entering

"Mr O'Toole madam" and ushered Seamus in

Mrs Jenson had a small vinegar face complete with two very small eyes like dark buttons and was in her seventy's looked at him with distain, as he approached her small eyes narrowed as she took in his peasant appearance

"Mrs Jenson"

Seamus said holding out his hand

"how do you do"

the old lady ignored his hand picked up a magazine casually thumbing through it and said without looking at him

"what do you want Mr O'Toole, please make it brief I am expecting guests"

Seamus took a big breath put his hand down and said

"your manager bought out Branigan's place when he died and Branigan gave me five acres 15 years ago which I have worked since then. He and I were indaid great friends only ting ye see he went an forgot tae put it in writin and now yous hiv gone in bought the lot, my bit anall. He wants me off ye see in me with the crop tae bring in" so the words spoken tersely

"what has this to do with me"

"but, but he wants me off" he said

"I cannot and will not go against my manager; it's not my fault if you were stupid enough not to get it in writing so good day to you sir"

and just as abruptly she rang for the Butler to see him off. She spoke to the Butler as if he was no longer there

"tell Sarah to prepare meals for 12 Hoskins if you please"

and with that turned her back on Seamus who completely at loss for words followed the Butler out. His anger and frustration knowing no bounds

"the auld spalpeen" he muttered

"I knew it, I knew it. She is so miserable she wouldn't fart cause she can't find a use for her gas O'Lordy what am I going tae do, an whit about the Orphanage what indaid what will they do."

Seamus had for fifteen years taken a cart load each year of his produce free of charge to the Orphanage of St Bridgets, his anger welled up inside him thinking of curses and vengeance mind was going this way and that way coming up with nothing. He got off his bike and started walking, it was warm for the time of year, an Indian summer some called it,

"whit the Devil ahm ah going tae do"

He sat down holding his head in his hands but little did he know he was sitting in a Fairy ring

When a voice said;

"whit ails ye man ye should be sitting there that way like all the world wiz agin ye"

Startled O'Toole looked up and there sitting before him was on a fallen tree trunk was a little bearded man dressed all in green

"and who are you" asked O'Toole

In answer to the small man's question

"me sur I'm Cornslip and you Seamus O'Toole to be shure" he replied "and what's yir problem that ye wid sit wit yer face in yer hans"

and so O'Toole told him his sad story

"mmm tis a tricky one" replied the little man

"for sur rightly be law thur right in rightly before justice thur wrong, mmm whit tae do wur ye thinkin uv vengeance be chance aye ah did Seamus replied

"mmm" said the little man again tinkin this is best for the council it's beyond mesel"

"now you sir are ye willin tae come with me on a little journey"

"Aye" said Seamus but me wife whit will she be thinkin to be shure the lord knows whit will go troo hur hade och content yersel"

replied the little man "shure an weel make time itsel stand still till we git back"

"Follow me sur" said the little man

As they took the path through the trees which sloped upwards to the high hills coming out of the small forest they were confronted by a sheer cliff wall rising a few hundred feet, the little man raised and pointed his hawthorn stick, a lightning flashed from it, and suddenly the cliff walls opened to reveal a small cave in the distance.

Seamus could see a bright light

"come Sur"

said the little man, and without waiting to see if he would come entered the cave. Gathering all his mortal courage Seamus followed him. Immediately, the entrance closed behind him and strangely enough it kept closing as they moved forward as if following them, sheer rock seemed to flow. The tunnel was lit by a strange light which seemed to come from the rocks themselves, then rounding a bend the sight nearly took Seamus breath away. Before him stretched a huge valley with many flowers and huge pine trees with a sprinkling of giant red woods, but it was the houses built in every shape imaginable, on one huge tree he counted three houses shaped like shoes others like boots, rabbits, bears and horses, not one house the same. The valley floor filled with laughing children the very air filled with their sweet music. To his right he spotted shops and a school sitting on the hill with a large playground, there were small carriages pulled by tiny horses, the place seemed to be a hive of industry.

"with all your magic why do you have to work" Seamus asked Corncrake

"ah sur to be shure its because we have to purchase our magic power, shure ye git nuthin fir nuthin in any world" Corncrake said

"I see you's all have beards" Seamus commented

"except the children, ah tis yer head is filled up with questions for ye see sur for one year in a Leprechauns life he has to wait a tousan years to a mortals one meself now I'm 64 years old Lordy" said Seamus

"you mean 64000, daid now dats the truth" said the little man

"but why are you helpin me instead of looking after your own self" asked Seamus

the wee man stroked his beard thoughtfully,

"the truth of the matter is me heart is to soft for me hade shure the council will not be pleased at all at all" he replied "bringing ye here oh to be shure here they come" he continued

The children had spotted them first, they were dressed all in green and started dancing around them, Corncrake laughingly shoeing them off as they headed down deeper into the floor of the valley, then before them a small building with many turrets and spires

"that's where we be going, it's the council chambers"

The beauty and splendour of the valley had fair took Seamus's breath away and in a few moments they crossed the threshold, the door was swung open by a small bearded figure who looked grim faced

"you've done it again Corncrake" he said

"this time you could be in real trouble"

Seamus glanced at Corncrake and indeed he did look kind of nervous

"it is not his fault" Seamus said quiet

"mortal this is not your domain" was the answer

They entered a larger room with a huge table, seated around about twenty small men All looking rather grim faced a voice spoke from the head of the table

"Corncrake to the centre of the room"

Seamus's legs could not move as the little man walked slowly forward the voice boomed again

"you know the rules, this is not mortal domain"

speaking slowly faltering a little Corncrake told them Seamus's story and how he did not know what to do.

"I have enough magic power left to erase, his memory" he told council "that is why I brought him to you, that you may find an answer to his problem"

the head Leprechaun then spoke to Seamus

"what sir have you to offer for any favours given to you?"

"I will sur share a quarter of my crop wit you and I will" said Seamus excitedly "for the rest of me life"

the council huddled together then said

"Corncrake take the mortal outside till we confer"

Outside they sat in the warm sunshine for about ten minutes before they were recalled

"Corncrake we have decided that you will go back into the mortal world and see what you can come up with to help this man, you will reduce in size and be kept in the mortals pocket, you can in this way send us a picture of what is happening, you can be free to use your own discretion in all matters and deal with this problem" the head of Council said

The council now were all smiles

"take the mortal and show him our village, make him feel at home but be sure to remember not by word or deed must you tell anyone of us or terrible evil will befall you"

"He agreed heartily dade sur I do, not one word, not a soul not even me own wife" said Seamus

and with that Corncrake said "come and meet my People"

It was indeed a place of enchantment cobblers blacksmiths dressmakers candle makers miners and bakers just to name a few, the time flashed by as the leprechauns entertained Seamus, too soon it was time to go and they made their way back through the tunnel. It opened as before then closing completely, one flash of light and Seamus again stood before a bare cliff wall, just as if had been a dream and Corncrake had disappeared. Then Seamus heard a voice coming from his top pocket;

"Tis me" said the voice

It was Corncrake

"Seamus now this is how we will git around, furst me son lets go meet yer good wife" he said

On arriving back at his home his wife was very eager to hear his news "well" she said

"what did the auld biddy say" she asked

"say, say, the oul witch" replied Seamus "shure she made me feel like I wis a bit of durt that she had scraped off her shoes" he then told Nessie of what had happened at the big house leaving out nothing,

"what are we going to do" she asked

"oh I'll tink of sumfin, but furst woman me dinner before I starve tae death"

Nessie smiled to herself

"thank the Lord he is not takin this as bad as I thought he would" she thought to herself. So she went into the kitchen to put out his dinner a small voice said on

"yer saucer is mine Seamus, us little people eat to ye know"

Seamus grinned

"to be shure to be shure" he said.

The following morning Corncrake ate a hearty breakfast how he did this was quite ingenious, he had discovered an old clock on the shelf which had a large space behind it, he got Seamus to set up a small tin for a table and a match box for a seat and his plates came in the way of sea shells, a lid from a bottle served as a cup and when Nessie had gone into the kitchen Seamus served him his meal,

"Begorra Seamus I have an idea the furst ting we must do" Corncrake said

"we must lift yer crops, shure people will buy the lot from ye remembering of course our 25 per cent" he explained

"dade now tis a good idea" said Seamus "but they will stop us for sure"

"dade now sur that they won't, you just leave it to me" the little man replied before vanishing.

Three hours later he reappeared with a big grin on his face

"begorra, its to be done tonight all me people will lift the crops and tomorrow the ground will be bare" Corncrake explained

Well next morning Seamus walked by his field very early and sure enough it had been stripped bare even the waste stalks had been burnt, the land was as clean as a whistle.

He was not long home when Seamus heard the roaring noise of his visitor, twas the man himself O'Roirdan, he battered the door with his stick. O'Roirdan stood there his face flushed with anger "ye lifted yer crops" he said

"dade sur ah did not" replied Seamus

"ye did, ya scoundrel, al have the law on ye, you'll not get away with this" O'Rourdan bellowed

With this and brandishing his stick he stocked off.

"now sur we will have a little fun" Corncrake grinned

"fun? More like me being in the jail" said Seamus

"now, now, content yersel man, jist trust me, when they bring the law say show me the field" Corncrake told Seamus

A half hour past and O'Rourdan again turned up but this time with the local Sergeant Murphy

"Sargent! arrest this scoundrel" he demanded "he stole my crops"

"what have you to say for yourself Seamus?" Murphy quizzed

"Drivel, ah tink he's talking drivel" Seamus replied "let's go and see the field"

He put on his cap and his jacket and off they went down to the field and so help me everything was as before, all the crops looking very healthy indeed,

"whit nonsense is dis" cried Murphy

"but, but it was empty this morning" O'Rourdan said puzzled

"och man, your working too hard, yer havering" said Murphy "sorry to have troubled ye Seamus"

O'Rourdan stood there scratching his head, he turned and walked away muttering, not even a single glance at Seamus, who was looking down at the wee man in his pocket and tiped him a wink, the little fellow once again pointed his stick at the field and again all the crops vanished

"where did you get them" Seamus asked

"shure now from the field up the road, I just borrowed them fir a short time" Corncrake said as they both laughed.

"Now" said Corncrake "in your top drawer is the money for the crop minus the 25 per cent, you will find we gave you top price and no charge for the labour

Seamus thanked him and they both set out contently

smoking their pipes in quiet companionship as they strolled home,

"you know Corncrake, he will be back fur shure"

"dat he will" replied Corncrake "but a don't tink he will sendin fir the law. Dat I know"

On the way down to the pub they passed Mrs Mullegan's house. She was hanging out her washing and her baby was crying "mornin Misses, how are you dis mornin" Seamus said

"shure the chiles makin a fuss to be shure" she replied

"me man in I hiv nut been gittin much sleep since the day he wiz born, ah don't know whits like the matter with him" she continued

Meanwhile Seamus could see what she was talking about, the child girned all the time.

"go over to the chile and put yer hand on his head in say, der now dat will do ye" Corncrake whispered in Seamus's ear

Seamus complied with the command and as he did so the child ceased to cry but instead started to gurgle with delight

"glory be to God" the woman said "shure you hiv the touch of a saint, oh Lord, Seamus, thank ye so much"

As she clasped her child to her busom Seamus said

"Shure tis nuthin attal attal"

And walked away whispering quietly to Corncrake "shure to God ye hiv a kind heart"

Meanwhile things that had been going smoothly in the village now a change was on the way in the shape of Corncrake who with Seamus having his spending money went down for a pint and sure enough Corncrake liked a dram himself, but lordy how it affected him, it turned his head completely. The village men had gathered for they too had heard the story told by the Sargent and O'Rourdan had the butt of quiet a few jokes before Seamus and Corncrake arrived. Seamus held his pint of Guinness up at his top pocket for Corncrake to sup away happily.

Shortly after things started to happen

O'Rourdan struck a match to light his pipe, it caught fire right away bursting into flames

"in heavens name man" said the blacksmith Ricky Doherty "whit have ye in yer pipe?"

With his hands shaking O'Rourdan called for a large whiskey and as he lifted it in his hand, Corncrake moved his little stick and it seemed to everyone that O'Rourdan poured the whiskey over his still smoking pipe

"wit the!" said the barman "are you alright?"

"I'm alright" O'Rourdan snarled in reply

As the place convulsed with laughter. How Corncrake achieved getting his whiskey down him Seamus did not know but he paid his way in the pub that night. M Sweeney behind the bar just scrathed his head and muttered to himself "ah tink we hiv mice in the till begorra"

But as the night wore on it went largely unnoticed. Meanwhile over in the corner of the pub sat Joe Evans, they called him the pig man for he had over 300 pigs and he sat himself most of the time. A very dour man, not mixing with the locals, he had come from England over 30 years ago after working in Dublin. He saved his money and bought out the original owner, McGin. Coming down to the pub was his only recreation, unmarried; he was not a very civil person, liking his own company. The men of the town giving him a lot of space, the most he muttered was "another pint"

To the barman, then back to his seat. Anyway just after the O'Rourdan incident, Evans, now on his fifth pint, went to the bar. He was tall and lean, the scowl always evident on his face said "pint"

The barman drew him one and he walked back to his table, as he sat down the chair drew back itself and he and his pint crashed to the floor. The pub erupted with laughter, Even's not seeing the funny side of it scrambled to his feet, his long skinny face glowing red, as the barman walked over with his brush and mop

"bejabers, are you alright, shure you could hiv hit yer head in all, bejabers, yer lucky" he said

Seamus heard the wee man laughing and he knew who had caused the mischief. As the barman said

"com sur yel, have one on the house"

He never seen the till open and close so much as the wee man paid for Even's drink

They were both quite merry as they made their way home unaware of some of the comments by their friends in the bar

"I tot Seamus would be takin dis ting badly, shure ye niver kin tell kin ye"

Their was murmurs of agreement from his pals

Seamus wife God bless her had made a big plate of soup meanwhile the bold Corncrake had got rid of the emergency sea shells matchboxes etc, now there was a small bed stool, cups and plates making himself right at home so to speak, and tucking into Nessie's soup in that little place he had made for himself behind the big clock; Seamus grinned up at him

"shure and bejabers its fine soup is it not" before he could get a reply his wife spoke from the kitchen

"what's that your after saying Seamus"

"ah tis nothing, nothing attal cept it's a fine soup dat you make"

One hour later they were both asleep just before he dropped off he muttered

"I wonder what tomorrow will bring?"

The following morning the wee man vanished, Seamus gave the poke of gold coins to his wife telling her he had sold his produce telling her to say nothing to anyone, she was delighted

"tanks be to God" she said "I was worried sick about it not knowing when the next penny was coming from"

"och be jabbers" said Seamus tipping his nose with his fingers "shure ye knew I wouldn't let you down"

They both laughed as he gave her a big hug.

Meanwhile Corncrake was now at Mrs Jennings looking round a beautiful house with many extensions, each of the four corners were turreted a small pool with gold fish at the side of the house with huge lawns and a high wall gave shelter to the house and the vegetable gardens. To the right of the house was the stables setting it off very well

"Dade now" muttered the wee man "thurs money here dats fir shure"

Mrs Jensen had six guests staying at the house, retired Colonel John Williams, Mr and Mrs Holmes and her son Sydney and Mrs Lawson and her daughter Alice. Mr Holmes was a successful builder in England and as Corncrake stood and absorbed this scene a gong rang from inside the house calling them to dinner. So in went Corncrake they were all seated around a huge table in the dining room, the Colonel had a monocle which screwed on his already lean face pulling on one side of his face muscles. He spoke with a distinct lisp in an overbearing manner, he was 78 years old and his family had pushed him onto Mrs Jennings who herself was trying to prove to the English aristocracy that though she lived in Ireland she was every bit as good as them but to say the least he was a tiresome old fellow whom, she would love to see the back of. Mr and Mrs Holmes had shoved themselves on her as they had previously met her at a party in England, Mr Holmes was a thin man going bald, his wife was about six foot three and very thin she unfortunately had a very bad habit of repeating herself which was quite annoying and did not like Mrs Lawson's daughter Alice, whom she picked on constantly. It was indeed nothing but downright bullying, Mrs Lawson was a school teacher, small, and slightly plump with an attractive face. Her daughter Alice aged about 12 years with long black hair in pleats seemed quite happy except when Sydney was around, the old boy was sounding off at the table with a roaring stilt to his voice of his time in the army, no one was really listening as he reached for his glass, his wine tipped onto him he muttered angrily. When he had dried himself assisted by the waiter, the plate of soup tipped as he almost seemed to touch it and this time his trousers were soaked

"are you all right Colonel" asked Mrs Jensen

"do I look alright lady" he replied wrathfully

she was taken aback by his manner

"I beg your pardon Colonel please don't speak to me in such a manner" she said

He did not answer but threw down his napkin

"excuse me, I must change" he said

the servant cleaned up the mess as Corncrake grinned. Meanwhile Sydney was kicking Alice under the table who was looking very unhappy, Mr Holmes turned back to his food and his elbow caught Sydney smack in the face who then slumped momentary into his soup

"oh Lord son" said his dad "sorry here" producing a large white hanky

"no harm done Sydney" his face dripping looked like he wanted to kill, his eyes caught Alice grinning, his lips formed the words—I will get you later. Her face blanched

"dade ye? will ye now ?" said Corncrake "we will see bout dat"

An idea had formed in Corncrakes head these unpleasant unwanted guests must be got rid of promptly. He left the dinner table to its occupants to explore further when he encountered O'Rourdan talking to a well-built young man the same age as Sydney it was his son he was telling him to tell his mother he would be late for dinner, the boy very strong looking like his dad, red headed, about five foot five, 14 years old, the same age as Sydney. Corncrake grinned mischievously, one turn of his stick and he was back in the dining room whispering into the ear of Mrs Jenson. She in turn spoke to Holmes,

"I have been thinking about your boy" she said "he needs a companion, someone of his own age to play with. While he is here my foreman's boy is of the same age, he would, I believe, make him a good companion"

Corncrake smiled as he had implanted the thought in her head

"aye that would be fine" replied Holmes

"send for Mr O'Rourdan and ask him if he could attend me please"

"very good my lady" the butler replied

Five minutes later the butler came back

"Mr O'Roirdin is here maam"

He came in holding his hat in his hand

"you wished to see me maam" he asked

She quickly explained to him about his son

"shure, tis no bother attal attal" he said "would ye be wanting him tae come here everyday?"

"no indeed not" she replied "I will have a room set up for him here, he will become one of my guests"

0'Roirdan smiled "I will go tell him maam, he will be havin his dinner first now"

"Thank you Mr 0'Roirdin that will be all" with that he was dismissed

Young Sydney sat there at the table his face a picture to say the least thinking who is this scruffy boy son of the hired hand I have to play with. Meanwhile Corncrake sat back and grinned.

Two hours later young Danny was being shown his room, he looked a picture of dejection when he had unpacked, he was hustled off to see Mrs Jenson; her thin vinegar face holding a smile which did not reach her eyes

"it will only be for three weeks Danny, just look after him the best way you can, but remember show him your mettle boy, he is spoiled so I will leave it to you to make him understand our way of life. do you get what I mean Danny?"

"yes maam indaid I do" he grinned

"Hoskins will arrange for you to meet him" and with this she rang her little bell

Meanwhile, Corncrake had seen it all

"boy oh boy, now bejabers we will hiv some fun like" he said to himself

The butler Hoskins left Danny in the main hall

"Wait there son" he said and brought down Sydney.

He introduced them and left them to it.

"let's get one thing straight" said Sydney

"haughtily I did not want this, it was forced on me is dat so" replied Danny

"well sur now dis is the way of tings" and with that he grabbed Sydney by the scruff of his jacket pushed him against the wall and said

"you sur will do everyting I say and ye say nuttin tae nobiddy cause iffin ye do al punch the flamin lights out of ye ivery time ye open yer gub" he then shook him, Sydney his face bright red and near to tears shook his head in saying

"ok, ok"

"remember" Danny said "I'm di boss now lets get out of dis house it's to big fer me c'mon weve tings tae do" and with that he pushed Sydney out of the house

Corncrake grinned "auch to be shure tis a man he will be makin of him" and then he was off again to see what mischief he could get up to

He made his way into the cook house at the bottom of the big house where he found the wee crabit cook laying her weight and her voice around her moody. Mrs Mullen everyone was afraid of her as head cook she had been with Mrs Jenson for over thirty years and when the lady of the house spoke to her shure butter would not melt in her mouth but down here in her own domain she indeed was a very spiteful lady.

"Mmmm" came from Corncrake

poor Katherine McCarthy A thin small girl looking decidedly unhappy as the cook vented her anger on her calling her quite a few choice names.

"shure tis a sad piece of work ye are" Corncrake muttered and pointed his stick at Mrs Mullen. She started to stutter quite badly and the more she shouted the worse it got,

"oh be jabbers" she said slowly

"what in the name of God is happening to me" she looked angry and tried to speak to the girl but words would not come out. The maid ran and got her a glass of water putting an arm around her, speaking soothingly to the cook, she calmed down took a sip of water

"tank ye Kathy" she said, the words came out with ease

Another twist of the hawthorn stick the cook said

"leave all the dishes to me you go and lie down Kathy"

the girl could hardly believe her ears and she was shooed from the kitchen by the cook who then rolled up her sleeves' and started on the huge pile of dishes, pots and pans

"bedaid, sur" said the wee man "shure thurs always an answer"

with that he moved on. Meanwhile Danny and Sydney met up with young Alice and she took to Danny right away, there would be no more shenanigans, from now on Alice was safe.

Meanwhile the Colonel was in the drawing room smoking a large cigar when Mrs Holmes entered the room Corncrake gave the stick a twist words poured from Mrs Holmes mouth

"Would you please put that cigar out Colonel, I'm choking on the fumes"

"indeed you are good lady" he replied

"go open a window, or for that matter go for a walk, a gentleman needs his cigar after dinner" he replied she was very angry with his retort her, working class background now came to the fore

"is that right—you miserable old man, how would you like me to light up" she said he in turn looked at her in amazement

"pon my word, you are a cheeky bitch, but you go ahead and have a cigar" she took one from the box and lit it, from one of the candles and proceeded to blow smoke in his face. The room quickly filled with smoke as the Colonel got angrier

"damn you woman" he said "damn you"

As he got up and stormed of the room. Mrs Holmes sat down weakly in her chair putting out the cigar she felt very sick indeed, rushing out of the room to the toilet where she was head down over the pan vomiting—the whole house could hear as Corncrake laughed quietly to himself

Things were not going well for young Sydney as Danny asked him to help with the lifting of the potatoes. Lord his back felt like it was broken but he was so afraid of Danny he just worked on thinking "can't wait to get back to the house and ask daddy to go home" this thought kept him going

Meanwhile the Colonel went for a walk, one little tap from the stick from Corncrake and flies and wasps were buzzing around him. The poor man he was in a right state when he returned to the house.

"I am leaving tomorrow Mrs Jenson, I cannot stand this place another day" he said

"Oh dear" she said "we so enjoyed your company" he mumbled something and went into his room to pack

"one down tree to go" said Corncrake

Mrs Jenson met Mrs Lawson in the drawing room and asked her to go with her and Alice for a drive in the chaise

"oh that would lovely" she replied

"good, then we will leave after supper if that's ok with you"

"by all means Mrs Jenson, we will delighted"

So directly after supper they set off, a big black horse pulling the small chaise

"here" Mrs Jenson unburdened herself to her friend

"oh dear" she said "the Colonel is going home ? I don't know what his family will think of me?"

"I would not give it another thought" replied Mrs Lawson "they pushed him on to you and he was to say the least a very rude man" "hmm, I do believe Katherine you are right, but we still have those horrible people, the Holmes—oh dear I do sound quite awful but they are rather wearing don't you think"

"indeed I do" replied Mrs Lawson "but lets look on the bright side they cannot stay for ever" and they both laughed

Meanwhile Corncrake, was taking a good look around the large house with its many extensions, it was in the stables he overheard the man in charge, big John McGuire say to one of the stable lads

"now you make sure dis little filly gets good taken care of when I go down to Takismore fur di hoss sales, she be thuh pride in joy ov Mrs Jennings, dade sur she is" he breathed

"now ders ah ting" thought Corncrake with a mischievous glint in his eye.

As night fell Corncrake appeared right at the elbow of O'Toole just as he was about to swallow his pint

"begorra" he said, "you gave me a fright, I tot it was my guardian angel comin fir me soul" at that he crossed himself

"and say, you nuthin sur an git me up a pint of dat luvin black stuff" O'Toole groaned

"shure tis yer crock of gold am supposed tae find tis mah crock of gold yer drinkin" but it was only Irish humour as indeed Corncrake knew well

"who was dat ye wur talking tae O'Toole?" ask the barman "bejabers, ah tink you have lost your marbles" he said as he slid a pint over to him grinning "am after to begittin worried about ye sur" and went back to serve someone else

"you sur?" said Corncrake "will be getting a call from the office"

"wit me?" stuttered O'Toole quickly he wiped the froth from his mouth and pretended to cough and splutter

"ach" he said to all and sundry "ah near choked it went down the wrong way yid tink by tis time the damn stuff wid know where to go!" and they all laughed then he muttered to Corncrake

"ahm goin down der fer what oh says he spects it will be a sick horse fer shure" said Corncrake

"I must find that love that's in her heart"

Back at the house young Alice was in the drawing room, Mrs Jenson looked up and smiled

"hello Alice, how are you this morning?"

"very well thank you Mrs Jenson"

"that's a lovely dress you have on Alice, it really sets your red hair off very well"

Alice smiled shyly

"would you like to go for a walk it's so very lovely outside Alice"

Alice said "yes indeed I would Mrs Jenson" as she rose, patted her hair lifted her cardigan and said

"let's go Alice"

Taking her hand they moved out of the house

"let's start at the stables, I have something to show you" said Mrs Jenson

Sean the head holster tipped his cap

"mornin Mrs Jenson"

"morning Sean, this is Alice, we have come to look at the new colt"

"with pleasure maam" he said "follow me"

Around the corner was a small paddock and there the mare and her lovely colt; jet black with a small splash of white on its forehead.

"oh its beautiful" Alice breathed

"you like it" said Mrs Jenson

"oh yes" Alice replied her eyes dancing in her head

"she is yours" said Mrs Jenson

"you don't mean, it's mine! oh but it's too much, mummy would not let me take him"

Mrs Jennings smiled

"its ok I told your mum yesterday, she was delighted"

"oh thank you Mrs Jenson, thank you so very much"

"you will have to give your colt a name, what will it be ?"

Alice looked at the colts lips pursed then said

"I will call him Star for the star on his forehead"

"now" said Mrs Jenson "John will teach you to ride and how to look after him. You must come down every day and soon you will be really good friends"

"oh I will I will" Alice replied as she patted the young colts head

Corncrake noted how the old lady changed from being Vinegary while in the young girls company

"mmmm" he said thoughtfully "so di lady has a heart"

Back at the house things were livening up as young Sydney got back to the house he tottered wearily up to the door of his room then changed his mind going towards the door of his parents room without knocking he burst in shouting

"mummy mummy, I want to go home" his mum was at that moment regaling her husband with the story to her somewhat startled husband of the incident with the old Colonel, unaware that the old gentleman was leaving

"what the devil is the matter boy" his father exclaimed the boy lamented the story of the potato lifting

"that's it we are going home" his mother said "what with that grumpy old man and now this"

"but wait" protested her husband "we can sort this out"

"indeed you will not my man, we and here" she put her arm around dear Sydney who smirked at his dad

"we have had enough"

"oh very well dear" he replied "I will go see Mrs Jenson and tell her we are leaving"

"right" was all she retorted glumly her husband departed to convey what he thought was bad tidings to Mrs Jenson

"go and get washed up Sydney and start packing" she said as he left as the boy left the room he spotted young Alice going into her room, she in turn seen him covered in mud and could not hide a smile

"you little brat" Sydney shouted and started to run towards her. Unlucky for him Corncrake was there and observed his actions, Sydney was now running but unfortunately for him his feet were running on the spot as athletes say; his legs going like pistons yet pinned as it were to the floor quickly. Alice got into her room and locked the door suddenly Corncrake lifted the spell young Sydney, he shot forward like a bullet skidded on the polished floor and ended up head over heels in the corner unhurt but badly shaken. He got up and staggered into his room wondering what had happened to him

"dade now, some people niver learn" chortled Corncrake as he moved to another part of the house

The Colonel could be seen, his bag being put into the chaise, his farewell to Mrs Jenson were very brief then he was off. Once he was out of sight if one had looked they would have seen Mrs Jenson brushing her hands together as if to say thank the Lord I am rid of him for good, now she thought there is only three left to go, Holmes just then approached

"dear Mrs Jenson something has come up and we must be off at once, business you know" he then thanked her for the wonderful holiday they had and how sorry they were to leave. Mrs Jenson made the appropriate noises he wished to hear, she never said the Colonel had left as she did not want them to change their mind instead saying how much she had enjoyed their visit but indeed one must do what one must do

"I must go now and help my wife pack, we shall leave after supper if that's all right with you" he said "by all means Mr Holmes by all means" she replied he in turn hurried away unaware of the smile which was spreading over the old ladies face. Corncrake sitting on the branch of a tree clapped his hands

"begorra I'm not the brainy one" he chortled

A shout from the stables startled Mrs Jenson it was the head stable lad he came over looking very flustered indeed

"Oh Mrs Jenson the pony its took badly with the foreman away"

"send for Vet right away" she retorted she hurried to see the Colt and found it lying in its stall breathing very swiftly

"oh you poor thing, what have you eaten" she said stroking its neck

Just then Mrs Lawson and Alice came running up. Alice burst into tears

"Their their now" said Mrs Jenson "don't take on so I have sent for the Vet he will cure it indeed"

"he will" said Corncrake sitting on a spar near the box "indade he will shure the man must be a magician" he twisted his stick and vanished only to appear next to O'Toole

"shure to God ye almost gave me a heart attack"

Corncrake grinned saying

"now ders a ting hear now Seamus anytime in the next hour dey is going tae send fur ye"

"who ?" said Seamus

"di owl lady, who else?"

"ye tink man whit fur" said Seamus

"ah tis hur colt its gone an takin sick so it has in you bejabers wae all yir gifts shure your di man fir the job"

"whit in hivin ir ye up tae Corncrake?"

"ah sur jist a little bit oh magic yeel see" and he vanished

Meanwhile back at the stable the Vet had tried everything to no avail

"its beyond me" he said to Mrs Jenson

"the bloods clear, no swelling, eyes clear. I checked the stomach, it's not what it ate" he stood up scratching his head

"maybe the colt will come out of it by itself, I don't know" the stable lad piped up

"send fur Seamus O'Toole, shure he his di gifts he kin make him better so he kin" he hardly had the Words out of his mouth when Mrs Jenson said

"go at once and fetch him, take a spare horse and ask him to come at once"

Off went the lad to fetch Seamus and to be shure he was ready to leave right away. 20 minutes later he dismounted at the stable but before approaching the Colt, a voice in his ear said go o the Colt put your hands on its head and blow into its mouth then say up ye git lad up ye git. He walked over to the very grim looking group around the stricken animal, its body now going into spasms the Colt breathing very harshly,

"it's the Colt, its very sick. Could you please help" asked Mrs Jenson without replying Seamus got down on his knees put both hands on the Colts head

"this is superstitious nonsense" the Vet said

"be quiet sir" said Mrs Jenson "you sir could do nothing now please give the man his chance" gently Seamus stroked downwards on the Colts nose then stooping down breathed into its nostrils as he lifted his head he said

"up ye git boy ye are alright now" then Corncrake twisted his stick and the little pony opened its eyes lifted its head and struggled to its feet, gave itself a shake then pranced about looking very lively indeed

"oh my Lord" said Mrs Jenson

"it's a miracle" everyone echoed her as she turned to Seamus

"Mr O'Toole I was very rude to you when you came down to see me would you please forgive me?"

"oh dade now an dat wis nutin attal attal"

"but no" she retorted "I sir will make all things right" she said

"go at once and get Mr O'Rourdan ask him if he would see me right away" she said to the stable lad

"you sir you shall indeed have your piece of land for ever, what is right is right and it is yours. Would you be so kind as to come to the house for a glass of sherry and I will make out a deed of ownership to you" Mrs Jenson said

"tank ye kindly Mrs Jenson" Seamus replied then turned to Alice and her mother smiling

"would you please excuse me, I must attend to this business right away"

"of course" the both replied

Corncrake jumped up and down with glee. They had just entered the house as O'Rourdan put in an appearance

"Mr O'Toole will have his field back" she told him "you can be a witness, from today it is his for life"

"but, but" he skittered

"no buts sir, I will make him out a deed of right. You see that everyone in the village becomes aware of this"

Twisting his hat in his hand O'Rourdan hurried out to comply with her orders

"dat I will maam" he said "dat I will" she sent Seamus home on one of the mares with the stable lad to bring it back

"I am sure sir you will want to give the good news to your wife as soon as possible, and once again thank you sir for curing the pony" with that he was ushered out of the big house. When he had arrived at the door of his home and the stable lad was away, there waiting on him was Corncrake. They both jumped up and down with glee

"jumpin bejabers Corncrake, tank ye so much. How kin ah ever tank ye fir all yeve done?"

"ah sur remember di 25 per cent" and they clasped each other's hands. Just then a sad look came over the wee man's face

"whits di matter sur" said Seamus

"oh di jobs done now an al be after leavin ye"

"ah dae ye hiv tae go so soon ?"

"dade in ah have" the wee man replied but he then took a small gold ring from his finger saying

"if iver ye hiv need o me jist give it tree twists an I will come maybe even fir ah sup"

And they both laughed

"shure in bejabers al niver be going to get that ring on ma finger" Seamus said

"och sur" Corncrake replied "give it a try" and sure enough it got bigger and slipped onto his finger no bother at all

"tank ye, Corncrake am going tae miss ye dat a will" said Seamus "I've got right fond of yer company, should ah come over tank di rest of yer people?"

The wee man shook his head

"no need attal, goodbye sur" both shock hands

"remember am niver far away" and with that he vanished. Just then Seamus heard his wife shouting and he hurried in to tell her the wonderful news

The End

THE LEPRECHAUN

A man full of troubles sat down on a stump
As he pondered the evil of what they had done
They had taken his field that he worked that year long
All the fruits from his labours had now all gone wrong
It was old Mrs Jenson who had bought his field and the works of his
labour was now hers to yield
Oh what will I do as he rattled his brain
When a voice said bejabers what gives ye sich pain
Seamus looked up and there sat on a tree
Was the smallest wee man that one ever did see
Dressed all in green with a cap on his head
As the voice said bejabers you look sur half dead
What troubles ye so dat ye look full oh grief
Tis now shure a fine mornin hey sur are ye deaf
So Seamus related the story in full
How Branigan died without leaving a will
Of the head man O'Rourdan and the part that he played
And of meeting Mrs Jenson and been shown the front gate
Now sur dats a problem the wee man replied
Ye come tae my home where sich answers supplied
As cliff walls they opened Leprechaun land it appeared
Hundreds of people and all men they wore beards
The committee was angry why did you bring here
As Corncrake explained all the problems appeared
They pondered then answered its all up to you
Go now with O'Toole and do what to do
So off both they went the answer to find
The Leprechaun must live with the mortal mankind
But by hook and by crook the answer was found
And Seamus O'Toole now owns Branigan's ground
To close read the story for you know it is true
In auld Ireland theirs magic just for me and for you
The Leprechauns are legend yet part of this land
So beware don't make cross a wee Leprechaun man

CPSIA information can be obtained at www.ICGtesting.com
Printed in the USA
LVOW12s1818030214

372115LV00002B/491/P